As Iron Sharpens Iron

By

Ruth Lee Alfred

Editing by Sarajoy Bonebright
Cover Design by Christine Busch

www.truthbyruth.com

~ Dedication ~

I dedicate this book to my military family, my church family, and my friends.

I want to thank my parents for my childhood experiences, and my best friend, whom is also my husband, for the encouragement to write this book.

Thank you!

~ Acknowledgements ~

USAF Chaplain Gabriel Rios

USAF Chaplain Robert Johnson

USAF Chaplain Eusebia Rios

ARMY Chaplain David Santiago (ret)

USAF Pilot, Wayne Black

~ **Table of Contents** ~

~ Preface ~

This novel is a great accomplishment for myself, not just because of the contents and real-life experiences, but because I overcame my fear of writing and not allowing my language barrier to stop me from expressing myself.

I simmered this story for a few years before I decided to write it down. Its true experiences serve as an inspiration and encouragement for others to truly see the hard work of our military service members and how our chaplains really devote themselves to the community in order to draw them closer to God.

CHAPTER 1
~ Medium Speed ~

Rebecca

"Yes, may I have one Oreo and one M&M McFlurry... with extra napkins please?" my mother asked.

A family ritual whenever we were to participate in one of my father's military or religious activities: Our mother would "treat" us to something delightful, like a deposit in return for good behavior, to keep us busy or rewarded for whatever we were forced to patiently endure. Most of the time, it was to wait for our dad at his office (in the chapel), which is where we were headed today.

Ever since I turned fifteen last week, I had become increasingly sensitive to a lot of situations lately. I started to see things more clearly and feel emotions differently. It was like I had put on glasses for the first time and could see things closely and with vibrant detail.

Of course, that all probably came from the rigid torture of my body changing and hormones flaring up and down. I will admit: I could be melodramatic and theatrical... but what teenager couldn't be? It felt like life experiences could be exciting again, and I was looking forward to what this passage had in store for me.

In the last year, I gained more responsibilities than I ever had before, and those experiences included some major life-changing events...

The first one was acquiring my driver's permit. I could drive! The downside of that opportunity was that I could only drive with one parent: my father. I refused to be taught by my mother. Even just by looking at the wheel, she could predict a crash. She even scolded me, calling me a bad driver, just because I brought the wrong keys to the car one time. There was no reasonable exchange of conversing with my mother, especially when it came to driving, because I had already been handed down a sentence before my trial had even begun.

The second significant responsibility in my life was applying for colleges and universities. That meant taking the SATs, prepping for tests, writing essays, and taking practice exams and after-school tutoring in order to be ready for junior year. If I really focused and applied myself, I could potentially graduate early.

The pressure was also on with balancing my academic and social life. I just hoped my family could be as supportive as possible, without any life interruptions, and that this season of my life could be a smooth, stable transition into adulthood.

Just a few minutes after leaving the drive thru, we pulled in the base entry and waited in line to be carded for access. The average wait time to get into a military installation was about 20-30 seconds—sometimes, even up to four minutes during busy hours. We normally could go right through, since work hours were usually 8am-5pm. With most people leaving, we could usually breeze right on through the gate. However, today, at 5:33pm, we were behind one particular vehicle that was taking a long while. After the average 30 seconds of wait time, I settled my spoon in the ice-cream cup and started to look up to see what the holdup was.

I noticed the guard looking down, submissively mouthing, "Yes, sir..." over and over again to the driver. I immediately began to investigate in my mind all the possibilities as to why we weren't moving and why she was repeating the same affirmation multiple times. Like I mentioned, the time to get into base after work hours was predominantly quick, and anything out of the ordinary felt like an eternity.

Finally, 20 seconds later, the guard saluted, and the man driving the vehicle in front of us drove off. We slowly pulled up to the young woman guard, giving her time to recuperate from whatever reprimand and humiliation she had just sustained. I could see her take a deep breath, while keeping her head down and trying to avoid eye-contact—her face red, making the freckles blend with the rest of her baby-fresh-looking skin. She didn't look any older than 20.

"Hi! Happy Tuesday!" my mom expressed in an overly cheery manner, as she presented her military ID.

The guard unexpectedly smiled and replied, "Never heard of that, but thank you... Happy Tuesday to yourself, ma'am."

My mother began talking to her as if she was her own daughter, giving her words of encouragement, while closely observing the rear-view mirror, monitoring to make sure no car was waiting behind us.

As a teenager, constantly dealing with emotions, I could tell the guard had a rough day, but my mother had mastered my dad's technique of killing with kindness and that enthusiasm spread like a contagious disease—or was it the medicine to destroy the spreading disease? I couldn't remember just then.

Finally, I heard the guard giggle and laugh at my mom's latest comment. I was mildly curious at what she had said, but as usual, I had tuned out at my mom's corny jokes. I realized that they had been conversing just as long as we had waited in line, and the energy had shifted from awkward to comfortable. I began to feel anxious, frustrated, impatient, and cranky, and I had an urge to use the restroom after devouring the ice cream.

"Thank you, ma'am. Have a good day!" the guard finally said.

"You too, honey!" my mom replied, as she rolled up her window and we started to drive away.

Of course, I couldn't help but mutter a snide comment under my breath. "That took forever..." I rolled my eyes, condemning my mom for making me wait longer than necessary to use the bathroom.

She reasoned that the time it took for the prior driver to throw her in a ditch and bury her was the time she needed to get the guard out and back to safety, that words could descend someone as well as 'elevate' them back up the surface and that someday I would understand, or something... blah... blah... blah.

We arrived at the chapel, and my mom pulled up and parked in the main section of the parking lot, where it was clearly a long walking distance towards the entrance, rather than the visitor's spot, which happened to be right next to my dad's car. I was about to make another snotty comment and ask why, when we had an entire empty parking lot to choose from, we couldn't park closer next to dad's car and only have to walk a couple of steps towards the chapel instead of nearly 80 feet... But I thought it through, and I decided I didn't want to hear my mother give another lecture, parable, or lesson.

My little sister woke up from her sugar-induced nap and yelled out, "Daddy!" in excitement, while quickly looking around to find her superhero.

Lily's emphatic innocence and childish humor could be refreshing at times. I wondered if I was ever that cute or naïve. As I grew, I became bitter, knowledgeable, corrupt—well, a teenager. It was like the reverse transformation of a butterfly. The mesmerizing beauty of purity slowly deteriorated with time and growth. For now, Lily was the optimistic, hopeful, flamboyant princess that lived sheltered in the tower of the castle, while I could be the overbearing, overprotective, fiery dragon that circled her.

At times, I envied her for her sincere tenderness and kind character. I was about her age when she was born. I had wanted a sibling (or so I was told) since I was 3, but then at age 6, I became complacent and was ok with being an only child. My birthdays and Christmases were overfilled with toys and gifts.

When Lily came along, I noticed a steep decline on gifts, clothing, time, and attention. At some point, I began to get 2-in-1 gifts, where I had to share with Lily or split whatever was given to us. I believe that's why I started to engage in sports—to immerse myself in a hobby where I could self-satisfy my entity without interruptions or having to share attention with Lily.

When I began piano lessons, she took piano lessons. When I was interested in dancing lessons, she took dancing too. I get it. She admired me and wanted to do the same things that I could, but I still would have appreciated my own talents and accomplishments being valued for once.

As we got out of the car, we walked into the quiet, empty, cold chapel. All the lights were off, as if no one was inside. I could hear my little sister behind me asking my mom, "Where's Daddy?" even though we hadn't reached his office yet.

The elongated hallway felt forever to walk through, and I noticed all the lights were out, including my father's office. My mother replied to Lily, "He's somewhere in here, I promise."

As I approached, I could hear the light, clacking sound of his ceiling fan that had a certain rhythm that I distinctively memorized. It was on medium speed, and I knew he was around and/or was due to come back soon, since he always turned off the fan when preparing to leave his office. Instead of going in or turning my head to quickly check, I simply kept on walking by, passing my father's office, since I presumed no one was in there.

This building was old, broken and torn; it surely needed renovation. I can distinctly smell the humidity and mold in the carpets. For a house of worship – it sure wasn't appealing.

Six steps behind me, I heard my little sister happily call out, "Daddy!" I turned around and headed back towards my dad's office to find him inside, sitting down. Before I began to even open my mouth and interrogate my dad, my sister arraigned him first. "Daddy, why are the lights turned off if you're in here?"

He softly replied, "I was talking to God."

She adorably questioned him again, while giving him a hug and a kiss, "Why didn't you close the door, Daddy? I thought you weren't in here."

Like an attentive juror, I watched him speak towards my sister, but distinctly preach, like we were a congregation. "My door is always open to anyone. Just because the lights are off, doesn't mean I'm not here. Sometimes, you just have to look for me."

My mother gave him a hug and a kiss as well, and I was last to routinely follow up. As I sat down on his patient-comfortable couch, my parents started talking about how their day went.

Sore from volleyball practice, I decided to lie back on the couch and shut my eyes to relax for a few minutes, until I rudely had my feet shaken off the armrest.

"So how was your day, Becca?" my dad asked me.

As I pondered why he looked distressed, I simply shrugged and replied, "Okay..."

The answer, not to his satisfaction, spurred him on to ask, "How was volleyball?" He got up and started to turn everything off in his office.

Again, I answered, "Okay."

It had been only "okay". Nothing of anything consequential had happened. I had waited awhile after school for my mom to pick me up after volleyball practice, waited in line for a McFlurry, waited forever to get in the military base, and then waited for my mother to finish her chit-chat with the guard. I was not in the mood to have a decent conversation with my father.

"I feel like I'm always waiting for something..." I mumbled, and then realized my mistake. I had unintentionally engaged him in conversation.

"Sometimes, life is like that, Becca. People always talk about the big or memorable moments in their lives: graduation, marriage, kids, a new job, etc. Most people don't talk about the waiting in between..."

I looked up at him and briefly made eye contact, just to judge how long this discussion was going to have to take. He continued, "There is a time and a season for everything, Becca. God can use the season of waiting to strengthen you and teach you what you need to know for when the big moments do come around..."

I sighed, only half listening. This wasn't anything that I hadn't heard him talk about before. "I know, Dad... I know..."

He noticed I was growing a bit agitated, so he simply retracted from asking questions, grabbed my hand, and walked me down the hall, as if he was giving me away to a groom. He gave me a kiss and told me to head towards the car as he locked up the chapel.

I walked 3 or 4 steps behind everyone else, as we walked back to Mom's car. After we all buckled ourselves in, I sat back to relax with a sigh. I was tired, sore, sweaty, and confused. On top of that, I always wondered why we had to go in to meet our dad at the chapel rather than him simply telling us at what restaurant to meet. It was a drag to drive to base, wait in line, park, and get out, only to then reverse the process and do it all over again. I didn't know the significance, and I found it quite imprudent.

After a few minutes, he finally walked towards Mom's car, came up to my passenger window, and said, "Follow me... I'm taking you guys out to eat!" with a hefty smile on his face.

On the drive, I felt guilty and embarrassed about the way I had talked to him earlier. I was also ever-so grateful, because I was starving! I thought we had to participate or interact regarding some event on base, and then we'd get to eat—I guess I was wrong.

We arrived at the restaurant. As we were seated, time began to slow down. Shifting my speed to medium, I did my very best to perk up as we all begin to 'elevate' each other from our holes.

CHAPTER 2
~ Instrumental Healing ~

<u>Rebecca</u>

Seven days later, as we carried out our weekly ritual again, it was a tiresome day. It felt like the day had gone by really fast, to my appeasement, and as soon as my schedule had finished, I transitioned back to being a dependent of my parents again, strolling along with their schedule.

"Yes, hi! Happy Tuesday! Could I have two Oreo McFlurries... with extra napkins please?" said my mother. (If you must know, today I had felt like trying an Oreo McFlurry—hoping to instigate the same nap my sister always delighted in). As Mom distributed the ice cream, she reached into her purse, pulled out her cellphone, and started to call my father.

"Hmm, I wonder why your father isn't picking up... Becca, text your father that we're on our way." My mother, a skillful teacher, who could somehow manage to educate twenty-two kids, cook three items at the same time, clean the house, drive us everywhere, and then some, still hadn't figured out how to text. I was used to being her personal assistant when it came to tending to her cellphone... as well as her IT technician and spell-checker. It could sometimes be a bother at first, but I got to use it to my advantage when I needed or wanted something—yeah, I could be greedy sometimes and an artful master at guilt trips.

I slowly took off my volleyball uniform and placed it in my bag as I grabbed my phone to text my dad that we were on our way. As we were driving, we still hadn't heard back from my dad. Normally, he was very good at responding right away, so I kept checking my phone for good signal to make sure I didn't miss it.

Twelve minutes later, as we were getting closer to base, he still hadn't responded. My mom asked me to call him again in case he hadn't heard his cellphone the first few times. I held down number 2 for speed dial, and I could hear it ring four times, then go to voicemail.

I knew the protocol: If you couldn't get a hold of him on his cell, just call his office. I hung up and tried his office line. It rang at least five times until I gave up—nothing. Great, Dad was probably talking to God on the toilet again.

As we approached the entrance, I noticed it was the same gate guard from last week, and she quickly began to smile as we neared her. With a little wave, she said, "Happy Tuesday, Mrs. Ramonda!"

My mother was surprised at her witty introduction, smiled back, and replied, "Happy Tuesday to you too!" They chit-chatted for about 20 seconds—yes, I counted to ensure last weeks' long wait wouldn't happen again. As we were driving away, my mother tossed in a "God Bless!" this time, over her shoulder, to let the guard know we were believers of faith.

As we were pulling into the parking lot, I could see my dad's vehicle in the "Chaplain" spot as usual (by the front of the entryway and next to the handicap spots). Again, my mother decided to park in the main section... far... from... the... entrance. Didn't she understand that I was sore from practice? Why did she have to make me walk extra steps, knowing it was after 5pm and NO ONE WAS HERE?

Intrigued to unravel the mystery as to why my father hadn't picked up any of our calls, I woke up Lily. Knowing that this seven-year-old had the ability to nap anytime, anywhere, I unbuckled her and decided to pick her up. I threw her on top of my shoulders, piggy-back style, to carry her into the chapel.

We approached the hallway, and I could see that my dad had the door open and the lights were on, so we decided to launch a sneak-attack. As we got closer, we heard a woman crying. I immediately stopped and put Lily down to let my mother lead the way instead. I whispered to Lily to stay put, as I sped on my tip-toes to follow my mom. She stopped near the door, realizing that there was a counseling session with a distressed woman still going on.

My mom quickly turned around and clearly articulated with her mouth for me to turn around also. I stood motionless. She yanked me down the hall and sat us down in the front waiting area.

I had seen my father throughout my life talk to people anywhere and everywhere—from church to my school events, to grocery shopping (especially grocery shopping), and given the circumstances, comforting them too. I guess, like I had said before, it never really hit me until I started seeing things differently recently. I never remember seeing my dad alone, patting another woman on her back without my mother present. He was always very careful about even giving the possible appearance of impropriety.

Speaking of my mother, she had sat down next to me with Lily on her lap, talking on her cellphone with a friend just to kill time. She didn't seem distraught like I was, hence I was confused. I stood up... walked around... went outside... looked at the time... It had only been 6 minutes. Patience and waiting felt like an eternity.

I went back inside to approach my mother, and asked with an impatient sigh, "What's dad doing?"

She answered me quickly, "Obviously ministering to someone."

I started to dissect and play with the word "minister" in my mind. Min-is-ter. Talk, sit, listen, worship, pray for, but never had I associated physical touch as "ministering". If hugging someone was considered part of ministry, then my parents had ministered to us every... single... day.

I realized and remembered my father saying once that God gives gifts to every individual to use. Gifts could be tools, talent, instruments—anything that God gives us to use for His will (and feel His presence). I had yet to decipher my ministering gift. Lily's was probably singing; my mother's was the gift of encouragement and talking with other people.

Bored as we could be, waiting, we decided to walk inside the actual chapel and race in between the pews. We saw Bryan Doherty, the drummer, packing a few things from the altar. We waved a quick "hi", purposely trying not to initiate a conversation—he talked A LOT. He was a nice guy, feared God, but he was a bit bitter towards women from his last break up—from what I'd overheard my parents' conversations. I decided to play the piano, while Lily grabbed the microphone to sing along.

Hearing Lily sing her heart out, like she was a performer on American Idol, I guessed we had accidently made quite the commotion. My dad walked out with the woman, and he led her toward the side exit in order to avoid introducing us. She looked young, mid-30's, brown-hair in a bun, wedding ring on her finger, no earrings, and about my height.

As she closed the door behind her, my father hollered out to us, "I'll be right there!"

He quickly went back into his office to turn off the lights. He came out towards us while putting on his jacket and service hat.

"Sorry it took so long..." He gave us all a pleading look, kissed my mom's lips, kissed my cheek, and then Lily's.

As we exited the chapel, the young woman was still getting in her car. I watched her as she put her purse on the passenger seat and her hat on her side handle door. As she closed the door, her hat fell off the handle. I wasn't going to say anything, but Lily, behind me, yelled, "She dropped her hat!"

Lily raced towards the woman's car, picked up her hat, and knocked on her window with a big smile. The young woman looked down to see Lily and smiled back as she rolled down the car window.

"Thank you, little lady," the woman said warmly. "I would have gotten in trouble for losing this. Thank you!"

My mom had not seen the whole event, having been several steps behind us and lost in conversation with my father. So, as she exited the chapel, my mom could only see what appeared to be Lily "bothering" the woman my father had just been counseling. She quickly rushed to get Lily out of the woman's way. She took Lily by her hand and said to her, "She has to get going, darling... and it's time for us to go too..."

The young woman smiled up at my mother then. "Ma'am, she didn't bother me. She was being a helpful little lady..." An awkward pause commenced after that.

The young woman cleared her throat and added, "I'm Captain Bailey, and I'm so sorry I held up your husband."

As Captain Bailey turned on her engine, my mother replied, "No worries at all, Captain Bailey. After all, that's his job—"

My mother got cut off as Captain Bailey continued, "You have a wonderful husband! He gives superb marital counseling, and when he gives illustrations or references, he talks about you like you're the love of his life. It's so sweet."

My mother was surprised at her remark, but still placated her with a smile. "Aw, thank you! He is pretty astute."

My mother didn't know the circumstances surrounding Captain Bailey's counseling, so she tried to keep her reply vague. She waved goodbye as Captain Bailey rolled her window up and backed out of the visitor parking spot. Still holding Lily by the hand, we all walked towards our vehicle. I opened the side door, and we all buckled our seatbelts.

As we drove off to eat somewhere, my mother called my dad on the phone to ask which restaurant we were heading to, and although I could not hear his end of the conversation, I could kind of put two and two together about what just happened...

"So, Captain Bailey said you are a wonderful husband and that you talk very highly of me... Jordan, I hope you're not giving them intimate examples of our issues," my mother sternly warned. She paused to listen to his response, then asked, "So, he's verbally and emotionally abusive?" ...and that's how I put the pieces of puzzle together. Captain Bailey had an abusive husband.

My mother continued to listen to whatever my father was telling her, and she replied, "Poor dear, maybe we should invite them sometime for dinner..." She waited to hear his incoming reply. "Oh, you already did?!" my mother exclaimed, but didn't really seem that surprised. My father had this tendency to invite impressionable people over for dinner without checking in first with my mother.

He knew that the secret to appealing to people with giving guidance was food. I had heard him explain that most business deals were done over a "business lunch", because eating was a human necessity, and when you buy a client their meal, you're expressing the notion that you will take care of their needs and the wanted service at hand.

My father didn't want to be seen as a pastor, a rank, or a uniformed man in office; he wanted to be seen as an approachable friend/confidant. Anytime that he took on a couple that needed counseling, or anyone for that matter, he wanted them to see him as a husband and father first.

My father would always say, "To teach others, you must use actions and not only words." His approach was very simple and complex at the same time.

Having a meal with guests was like a double-edged sword. He would teach us (my mom, me, and my sister) the problems that others were going through and how grateful we must be for our things, like commodities, health, relationships, etc. He would also discuss with us about the need for patience when he was running late coming home from work, comprehension of his daily work, compassion towards others, and gratitude that our family was not in the same predicament that so many others were in.

For the invited guests, my father wanted them to see the love and care that we shared at home, like the food my mom laid out by cooking for them. He also wanted them to feel like they were important and that he would make time for them outside work hours. He wanted others to see that he loved his family and that family should always come first—after God, of course.

I didn't mind on occasion having others come over. It meant I had to dress my best, help with the extra dishes, help cook, put the food away, and well... behave. Of course, the extra work never applied to Lily, as her effortless charm hovered as sole entertainment for everyone.

CHAPTER 3
~ Dutiful Dining ~

<u>Rebecca</u>

After a long day, finally Friday evening had officially begun. We got home from my practice, and I started to unload my bags and get ready to shower. My mother rushed to the kitchen to begin cooking for Captain Bailey and her husband. My father arrived a few minutes after we did, and he rushed to his bedroom to change.

Typically, I enjoyed long showers, but as a standard procedure for invited guests, I showered military style—quickly but thoroughly.

As I got dressed, I heard my mother yelling across the house, "Jordan, did you get tomatoes?!"

My dad poked his head out of their bedroom doorway and hollered back to her, "I put them near the stove, Joanna!"

Taking a deep breath, I commenced a quick checklist of my wardrobe and appearance: Hair? Check. Eyes? Check. Armpits? Check. Legs? Oh my! I could grate about a block of cheddar on my legs. I quickly scurried to put some pants on instead of the skirt I had planned, and I yelled from my room, "I'm almost done! I'll be there in a minute!"

I felt my mom was about to ask for help. I knew it was brewing, so I initiated a confirmation of my arrival in order to avoid my mother's nagging. It worked!

As I came into the kitchen, she said, "Thank you, sweetie. Please start slicing the onions, tomatoes, and peppers, okay?"

I grabbed the sharp knife from the drawer, placed the cutting board on the counter, and began to slice the tomatoes in fine, uniform squares—then, the peppers and the onions too. I hated doing onions. Inevitably, they made me tear up, hence ruining my mascara and other makeup. As I finished placing all the ingredients for my mom to use in a bowl, I started to place the mats and dress the table—along with Lily's "help". She brought the napkins, silverware, and cups, but she placed them all over... everywhere... incorrectly. ((Sigh.)) I pretended to "watch" Lily to seem as if I was helping in some way.

I heard my father turn on the stereo system, and symphonic music lulled throughout the house. My father came in and helped my mom with the drinks, getting the ice out of the freezer, grabbing the elegant pitcher we rarely used (only for guests), and assembling it all together. The doorbell rang, and we all paused what we were doing and looked at my father for instruction.

My mother sighed heavily, loudly enough so my father could hear and see that he was culpable of rushing her cooking by inviting guests at a "reasonable hour". The argument had always been for him to stop saying, "Dinner will be ready at 6." Instead, he was supposed to say, "Dinner will be ready after or around 6." We normally would get home on Fridays around 5pm, and one hour was not sufficient time to shower, dress, and prepare for a grand meal.

"I'll get the door," my father said. My mother continued to exasperatedly cook.

My father looked at me for the nonverbal agreement to "take over and help your mother" expression. I nodded, and he left the kitchen to answer the door.

I quickly got up from the table and began to disperse the drinks.

"Hello, Chaplain Ramonda!" we could hear Captain Bailey exclaim all the way from the entry way. "This is my husband, Tim." I could hear a young man's voice, but I couldn't make out what he said.

My dad did the usual tour around the house to eventually end up in the kitchen and meet up with the rest of us. As we heard him near by—questionably showing the laundry room—I started to sit down at the table with Lily, and I began to whisper to her the disclaimer: "Okay, Lily, we have company over, so please do not yell, scream, burp, or fart. Always go to the restroom if you need to do any of these. If you behave, you get to have ice cream. Oh, AND if you don't embarrass me, you can play with my makeup, okay? Got it?"

The smirk on that seven-year-old was as mastered and prominent as a salesman.

As we heard the adults nearing their way into the dining room, Lily and I sat in our seats like well-behaved border collies and nicely groomed poodles. We were going to have to endure an hour of sitting. I gave her my Giga-pet (a small, digital device that let you care for an animal of your choice), so she could stay entertained while waiting.

We had to remember our manners, speak when spoken to, and smile warmly. But afterwards, we were free to go and do as we pleased—if we remembered to politely ask to be excused.

By the time all the adults were seated, I heard my father say, "Let us pray."

As I bowed my head down and closed my eyes, I couldn't resist taking a sneak peek at everyone, curious to see every person's "prayer face". My mom was a pro-prayer. She bowed her head, closed eyes, folded her hands, and silently mouthed words to whisper her prayer. If they gave out medals, she would win gold for sure.

My father put on a serious face. He clenched his cheeks upward and nodded his head like a slow bobble-head toy, affirming and accentuating his prayer. I looked at Lily, and as she had her head bowed and eyes closed, she took the opportunity to pick her nose.

Captain Bailey was still, with her eyes closed. She had this look of desperation on her face—as if her problem were already out in the open and was praying in despair that nothing would go wrong tonight. Her husband was sitting next to her, with his head bowed, but eyes open, blinking at the tablecloth.

I had observed that people who usually have their eyes open tended to not believe in prayer or what was being said. However, the gesture of having his head down showed that he at least respected the right to prayer.

As we dug in and self-served from all the dishes, I immediately went for my favorite: potato salad with diced apple slices. There were also buttery bread rolls, steamed white rice, and pulled pork to devour. I zoned out for the most part, but occasionally, smiled and nodded as if I were paying attention.

I scooted the potato salad closer to me to ensure that I could sneak in scoops throughout the meal talk... and a quick few more again when everyone was nearing finishing their plates.

As we approached the dessert round, I decided that this pause might be my opportunity to get up and ask if I may be excused. I learned that once you were standing up, they really couldn't say no. Even if they had never said no verbally, they sometimes had with just their eyes—but, not tonight. I waited for my dad to finish his bite, and I also inserted the voluntary gesture of bringing dessert.

My father nodded, and I gathered my plate and brought it in the kitchen.

Ordinarily, Lily and I were not required to stay for dessert. We were allowed to take a small plate to our rooms and sneak away. So, we did.

My mother got up to make coffee for everyone, and my father picked up around the table and gave a kiss to my mother, thanking her for the wonderful meal. I knew it was one of their psychological and sincere tactics—to always show appreciation of one another publicly. It sent a strong message of unification, appreciation, love, understanding, affection, and much more... depending on the couple they were sending a ministering to.

Finally, I was free of duty, and I resumed to chat online with my friends in my room. Of course, Lily was in my room, too, going through my stuff and playing pretend. I was still on babysitting duty until our guests left.

As it neared 8pm, I could hear them talking by the front doorway, and I noticed the last song on the CD my father had put on was finishing—like a magical two-hour time limit. Guests would leave right at the ending of the song.

I told Lily to put everything back and that it was time to go to her room. I decided to take a bathroom break. As I finished washing my hands, I realized that if I wanted to show my parents that I was the mature I adult I proclaimed to be, I should go and shake our guests' hands and say "goodbye" too.

I took a deep breath and headed towards the entrance. My father was mid-sentence, talking to them about the importance of communication. I waited for the right pause to quickly step in and insert, "Thank you, guys, for coming over. It was nice meeting you."

Captain Baily replied, "Thank you for having us on a Friday night. I know it must have been a burden for us to trample in here on your night off." She smiled directly at me. She seemed relaxed, relieved—as if a heavy weight had been removed from her shoulders.

Her husband was still, motionless, and passive, but he was polite enough to say, "Thank you, Chaplain and Mrs. Ramonda, for the dinner. It was delicious, and I appreciate you all having us over."

As they all shook hands and the ladies hugged, I stood by the entry hall to stare at the human interaction that just happened and psychoanalyze what was said during the two-hour dessert delight. Whatever it was, it seemed to improve Captain Bailey's disposition.

Perfectly timed or so it seemed, just as my father shut the door behind the Bailey's, the last song on the CD track faded...

CHAPTER 4
~ The Clock's Hidden Hand ~

Rebecca

One of my biggest pet peeves in life is being awoken from a deep sleep. Lord have mercy on the soul that wakes me up in the morning, for my wrath will be as bitter as an aged gourd melon. I've had multiple alarm clocks on a yearly basis, since I was pretty rough on them.

One thing I hated about Sunday mornings was my mother's voice, so loud... Walking through the hallways, she would yell, "Time to get up! Let's go! Church time!" My blood boiled as I fought my eyelids with all my might to not open, hoping this was a nightmare.

Normally, I only set my alarm to go off on Monday through Friday to wake me. My routine was a quick morning tantrum, rapidly going through the 5 stages of grief, and then reasoning and acceptance that I couldn't stay mad at an alarm clock and had to get up for school.

That was never the case on Sundays. I enjoyed my two days off from school, especially Saturdays, when I had the freedom to sleep in with no commitment. But Sundays, although I was appreciative, I didn't have to wake up at 5am in the morning (school started at 6:30am), I got the compressed satisfaction that I could sleep in another 2 hours. But, no matter what, on Sundays, I still wanted more.

Chapel morning services were divided into two, and as a pastor's kid, I had to attend both services. So, regarding resenting my mother on Sunday mornings for a few minutes, I made peace with it in my mind as I trudged towards the kitchen, but only because she had coffee and breakfast ready for us at the table.

My father would leave early sometimes to get a head start, and we would meet up with him at the chapel. However, today he waited for us—all three women. Indeed, he was a very patient man of God.

*****

As we pulled up to the chapel, I unstrapped my seatbelt and Lily's. I closed my eyes, took a deep breath, put my "church face on", and I started the countdown for lunch as I headed inside the chapel. Sunday dinner was always a pot roast that my mother had simmering in the crock pot with golden potatoes and sweet baby carrots.

Mrs. Blanca Wade, a middle-aged lady we've known since we've been stationed here, faithfully arrived at church early every Sunday to pray at the altar. I didn't know a whole lot about her, but from what my little attention span had contained from eavesdropping on my parents' conversations, she was a recent widow from her second marriage.

She sat up with a lovely smile, pouty lips, rosy cheeks... and baggy eyes. She tried to mask her true sentiments as we walked up to greet her, and she quickly gave me a hug and a kiss on the cheek. She smelled like strawberries and mint. I continued my walk towards the front of the pews.

My mother normally did the "greet-the-world" tour before the service started. She would go from pew to pew to greet everyone. As she finally got near to me, she gave me the look—the green light to commence the dispensing of the antibacterial gel and be ready for her to get situated into our pew, get oozed and sanitized.

Slowly and nonchalantly, she sat down next to me, and I fired away, squeezing a quarter size amount of gel onto her hands. I, too, lathered my hands to rid myself of all the hand sweat, germs, bacteria... ugh. As I shook them off to air out, I look down at my watch; it was time. We all stood up, and the morning service began.

*****

As the last prayer ended, hunger ignited at the thought of lunch. I raced towards my father's office, and I scavenged around for snacks. Being a pastor's kid fortifies independence for strength to cope, endure, and wait. It usually took about fifteen to twenty minutes for the members to walk out, talk to one another, greet my father out the door, and then lock up.

As I sat at my father's desk, I sipped juice I had found in one of his drawers. Lily sat on the couch playing with her purse. My mother came to the door and signaled to us that it was time to go. I could hardly wait for a heaping plate... with gravy! Ooh, I had almost forgotten about the gravy. This Sunday was going to be a good day.

*****

Monday rolled around with great insouciance and apathy. As I waited for my mother to pick me up from volleyball practice, I repeated to myself the chain of events that led me to being tired, sweaty, hungry, and lonely.

Finally, as I saw my mother pull up, I got up from the bench and gathered my sports bag and backpack. My mother was on the phone (as usual), and I shifted into auto-pilot. I sat in the passenger seat and let my thoughts ramble about the day, on our way home.

I could feel the crisp air settling in and my long, dark brown hair swirling around me from the breeze of an autumn wind. My favorite time of the year; fall was flawless. There was no summer heat, no winter chilliness, and no spring rainy days.

Fall was the season to relax and sit back as the year was ending, the holidays were about to begin, and everyone began to wind down for family gatherings. It also meant guaranteed weight-gain season.

Nevertheless, although this season was good for me, my sister, and my mother, it became a very busy season for my father. He received many requests for invocations, party events, chapel meetings, counseling sessions, and so much more. Plus, he always did his best to accommodate our out-of-town family members, when/if they arrived. It's funny how the holidays were supposed to bring families together, but it usually brought divisions and disagreements instead.

My father had requested Thanksgiving week off in order to enjoy a full week with his mother, who would be coming into town for the holiday week, so he was going to put in extra hours, working from 7am to 6pm prior to her arrival to show superior workmanship.

Last year, he left in the middle of Thanksgiving dinner due to an elderly veteran's collapse and subsequent rushing to the hospital. Fortunately, the old man was alright and just had a minor stroke.

Often, people forget that a chaplain not only tends to non/active duty members, but also to their spouses, dependents, widows, veterans, contractors, and anyone else that has access to a military installation. While the base may operate from 8am-5pm, chaplains are always needed to be on call. If an emergency occurred after hours and someone had to be rushed to the nearest hospital, the chaplain-on-call would be paged for any assistance. Regardless, there wasn't one Thanksgiving that I could remember when my father was home all day, because of his duty.

My mother had been preparing all week by buying all the necessary ingredients and items for Thanksgiving and my father's work activities. Usually there was a chapel Thanksgiving dinner, a squadron dinner, and other friendly invitations from people at work. (I wasn't kidding about the weight-gain.)

*****

As the Thursday before Thanksgiving neared, my father had been coming home late and was determined to continue to work late to insure a relaxed, stress-free, and uninterrupted upcoming week with us. He got home around 7pm, took off his boots, sat at the table and began to eat dinner alone (since we had already eaten). My mom sat with him, caressed his back, and asked him how his day went.

By the time he was done eating, showering, and getting his uniform ready for next week, Lily was already asleep. I had casually seen him for a few minutes before I had gone to my room to chat with my friends, but I decided to go downstairs into his room and be with him for a little while. I sat on their bed to merely acknowledge him with respect and say "hello". He continued to talk with my mom and me about how his day had gone.

By 8:30pm, he decided to sit on his sofa to relax, while channel surfing on TV. As my mother continued to talk, suddenly, his phone rang. My mom looked at my father with a slightly stunned look on her face, inquiring silently as to who could be calling so late.

My father got up and walked over to his phone, where it was charging, and read the caller ID out loud to us: "Sergeant Miller." He picked up the phone, and to his dismay, Sergeant Miller informed him that there had been an emergency and he could not get a hold of Chaplain Dubose, the wing chaplain and my father's boss. Chaplain Dubose was supposed to be the on-call chaplain for the weekend.

My father decided to call his boss's personal cellphone instead of the on-call cell to see if he could reach Chaplain Dubose and see what the issue was. The call lasted about 30 seconds, and as I saw my father hang up, his face was instantly consumed with outrage and disappointment.

My father looked at my mother and repeated what Chaplain Dubose had said to him on the phone, repeating verbatim, but with his own irate twist to the tone of his voice: "I'm sorry, Jordan. I had a beer or maybe two, and I'm not fit to drive or handle the situation. Do you mind if you take care of it tonight?"

My mom burst out, "What?! He's on-call! What was he thinking? He should know better not to have drank! It's not fair, Jordan." She paused for a moment, trying to calm down. Then, she asked, "Okay, well, what about Chaplain Simmons? Is he available to help?"

My father shook his head, while replying, "No, Simmons is on-call during Thanksgiving weekend. Besides, he had mentioned that he was going to take his kids out ice skating tonight."

My father began to get dressed again to get ready for duty, while calling Sergeant Miller back for details of the urgent situation. My mom quickly went to the kitchen and prepared him a to-go snack and a travel mug of coffee.

"Sorry, honey," he said to her, as he took the snack bag and coffee out of her hands. "The emergency is a suicidal Airman... with a family and a gun. I've gotta go." He kissed her quickly and rushed out the door with a little goodbye wave to me.

As she locked up after him, I could hear my mother praying from my room. She teared up and began to pray out loud, "Lord, protect my husband and surround the situation with your mighty angels..." and the rest became a mumble to me. Her sincere prayer was a heart-felt lamentation and fervent supplication for my father.

"Mom, is everything ok?" I asked quietly, peeking my head into the living room.

With a sad smile, my mom simply said, "Pray for your father, Becca. He, too, is most likely praying as we speak, asking God for guidance and wisdom on how to defuse the situation tonight.

I looked up and saw the living room clock; it was 9:02 pm. Time was such a strange thing. Sometimes it seemed to pass by so slowly, and in other cases, someone's whole world could change, just like that, in the blink of an eye.

Rushing, waiting, minutes, seasons, changes, plans... if I thought about it too long, it made my mind swirl. A wave of compassion for my father washed over me. His job really was quite difficult; although some chaplains work for the salary, and some are working under God's commission. Often, because I was lost in my own selfish thoughts, I really didn't fully appreciate all that he did for our family and for others.

"Look at the time, dear. It's getting late," my mom noted, as if she was reading my mind. "Why don't you go on to your room and just pray for your daddy there. I'm sure he will be fine and should be home later tonight."

She gave me a hug goodnight as I shuffled to my room. I knew I wasn't going to be able to sleep yet, but I decided not to chat online.

After I laid down on my bed, I stared at the clock's hidden hand. I let my mind wander to what the minutes had in store for my dad that night. I began to pray more earnestly, asking God to watch over him.

CHAPTER 5
~ Negotiations ~

<u>Jordan</u>

As I neared the gate, I saw five police cars blocking the entrance and waving at me to continue to the next gate entry, since the first one was closed. I knew this was where I needed to be.

I rolled down my window and flashed my ID. "I'm Jordan Ramonda, the chaplain," I announced.

Sensing the urgency in my voice, the officer nearest to me scurried over to my window, checked the ID, and yelled out, "Let him through!"

As I passed through the entry, there was a security officer waving at me to approach him so that he could brief me on the situation. I hastily parked on the curbside, got out of the car as quickly as possible, and ran over to the officer. The officer indicated that I should get into his car quickly.

Before I was even able to get my seatbelt on, the car was zooming around the corner and down an alleyway.

"I'm Deputy Sheriff Fresno, and I'm the law enforcement officer attached to this unit (Security Forces). Thank you for coming. We got a call from a neighbor stating he heard yelling and cursing. Looking out his window, the neighbor observed Corporal Robert Nunes waving a gun and, what appeared to be, arguing with his wife, Jennifer. Their son, Henry (3 years old), is also still with them."

Deputy Fresno took a slight pause and looked over at me to see if I was absorbing the information. I nodded at him to continue. "We rushed immediately to secure all parameters as we evacuated everyone from housing within a mile radius and put base on alert. It has been confirmed that it is a hostile situation and the weapon has been sighted—unconfirmed if loaded.

"Corporal Nunes has served 2 tours—4 months in Iraq two years ago and just got back from a 6-month deployment in Afghanistan. He has been diagnosed with PTSD, but has been waiting on treatment, having only gotten back a week ago."

As the vehicle came to a stop, Deputy Fresno unbuckled his seatbelt quickly and handed me a thick file. "Here's his file if you'd like to take a look at it. Meanwhile, please put on this bullet-proof vest and helmet, as I'll need you to help me talk to him and try to get him to release his wife and son to safety."

I took a deep breath and hesitated. "Sir, I'm not normally called in to negotiate. I'm the behind-the-scenes person to comfort and deal with an aftermath of a tragedy, not to prevent one."

Deputy Fresno responded, "Yes, sir, we're aware of that, but Nunes has stated that he will not speak with our lead delegated officer and has requested to only speak with a chaplain about his sins. Our top priority is to get his wife and son out, and I give you my word I will be next to you the entire time to ensure your safety."

I froze briefly, and adrenaline rushed through my body. I felt like I had been electrocuted. The zap of nervousness seared from my heart down to my tingling fingertips. I did my best to put on a brave face, and not let Deputy Fresno see my hands shaking, but I wasn't sure how convincing my bravado was. I did my best to focus on doing what I was told, as I geared up as instructed. Silently, I prayed for courage, wisdom, protection, and God's grace and mercy.

Having finished putting on the protective gear, I glanced at my watch: 9:52pm. Following Deputy Fresno, we approached a "Do Not Cross" caution tape barrier. Surveying the scene as quickly as possible, I observed several vehicles and officers, standing nearby, ready to enter the housing apartment at a moment's notice if instructed to do so.

A man approached me from my right. He was mid-sentence before I realized that I was the person he was talking to. "...dangerous situation, but we are going to get through this together. Chaplain Ramonda...?"

"Yes, I'm sorry. What were you saying...?" I shook my head and tried to focus past my heart racing.

"Let me start again. I'm Officer Peterson, the trained negotiator here to help navigate us through this dangerous situation. Just follow my lead, okay?"

"Yes, yes, okay..." I acknowledged.

I followed behind him like a lost puppy as we approached the entryway of the apartment. Behind shielded glass and surrounded by six security forces, Officer Peterson turned to me and nodded. I wasn't really sure why, because he didn't wait for any confirmation from me before proceeding.

Officer Peterson picked up the megaphone and spoke into it clearly and with authority. "Mr. Nunes, at your request, I brought a chaplain. He is here with me right now, and his name is Jordan. He's here to speak with you and hear you out, okay? Now, we're going to speak to you on the walkie talkie that was delivered to your door earlier, please pick it up now."

Through the window blinds that were cracked slightly, I was able to catch a glimpse of the man beginning to cry and weep heavily, and then he disappeared. There was a minute of silence before the walkie talkie crackled, and Nunes spoke into it. "I'm here," Nunes said with a shaky breath.

Officer Peterson handed the walkie talkie to me. I looked over it for a moment, trying to decipher all the buttons' uses. Having no idea what to say, I opened my mouth and words just came out. "Corporal Nunes, my name is Jordan. Is everything alright?"

Nunes snuffled and said, "Am I alright?" He gave a dry chuckle. "No, sir, I am not alright. I am a lot not alright. Please tell me, what's the whole point?!"

I closed my eyes, saying a quick prayer for the right words to say. "The whole point of life? It's to live it the fullest Corporal Nunes—to make the most of the moments you are given, to love God, to take care of the ones you love (like your wife and son there), and to find happiness."

"No, no, no, sir! What's the point!? We all just die eventually. Does loving God really matter? How could He let my brothers over there die? How could that be part of His divine plan? Why did I get to come home and not them? How we die doesn't matter! We all die! There is no point to any of this..."

My mind swirled with responses, but I thought it best to keep him talking. Something Joanna had taught me was when I wasn't sure exactly what to say to answer a question with a question to gain more information. "What makes you believe that, Corporal Nunes?"

Everyone could hear the whimpers of Ms. Nunes as she held their son tightly on the floor in front of the couch, shielding him from her own husband. I could see from the tactical mirrors that the security forces were holding that Ms. Nunes was rocking back and forth to comfort their child. I couldn't, however, see Mr. Nunes' face at all. He seemed to be pacing back and forth between the kitchen and living room.

Panting, Mr. Nunes replied, "I saw how people got slaughtered over there! Innocent men, women, the elderly, even... even..." He wept a few moments before continuing, "...children." His voice changed from sadness to anger as he said, "I'm going to hell regardless, Chaplain, but my wife and son here, they won't suffer, will they? They'll get to go straight to Heaven, right?"

As soon as he finished that sentence, the negotiator and I looked at each other with great fear. We both knew where that kind of questioning led. Deputy Fresno cued all forces to be ready if they had a clear shot at Nunes.

I realized in that moment that I needed to talk to him face to face. I took a deep breath and said to the negotiator, "Let me in. I know it's not protocol, but he needs to see me to take me seriously and listen. He's wrapped himself in his world. He's not seeing his wife's panic or the threat of any danger that awaits him out here. Please, let my presence be known to him." But Officer Peterson shook his head "no".

Speaking into the walkie talkie once again, I asked another question to keep him talking: "Corporal Nunes, what makes you believe you're going to hell? God's grace and forgiveness is 100% guaranteed right now if you so desire…" There was a 10 second pause, which felt like an eternity. I decided to put pressure on the sheriff and the negotiator and do what I knew was the right thing to do. "Corporal Nunes, may I come in and sit with you?"

Officer Peterson looked at me with disdain, and Deputy Fresno slapped the hood of the car and muttered a swear word.

One of the officers standing nearby, spoke up and said, "He's nodding confirmation, sir…"

CHAPTER 6
~ From Here to Eternity ~

<u>Jordan</u>

After a very brief pause and quite a bit of glaring, Deputy Fresno approved my entry, only upon the condition that an officer needed to accompany me. I agreed and instructed through the walkie talkie, "Corporal Nunes, I'm coming in now to speak with you privately, face to face. Know that I'll have someone behind me for our safety, but not with me, okay?"

I began my 10-second prayer to my Creator, asking for guidance, wisdom, courage, and complete manifestation of His spirit to pour over me. I asked for forgiveness and peace.

As they completed a quick check of my bullet proof vest, helmet, and sides, I took a deep breath and began to enter the doorway.

Through the door, I spoke loudly, "I'm here now, Corporal Nunes. I am going to open the door now."

As I slowly opened the door, I refocused my eyes to the dim lighting, and did my best to quickly survey the scene. Everything was broken on the floor—glass, pictures, plates... they were shattered all over the house. Nunes was pacing back and forth, waving the gun in rhythmic circles near his head. But, when he saw me, he stopped the frantic movements, lowered his weapon, almost out of respect it seemed, and bowed his head. He began to weep.

Ms. Nunes had moved to the floor near the dining room table. She was shaking and had formed a fetal position on the floor, protecting her son. With her body curved around him, the boy was barely visible—his small frame shielded. I couldn't hear what she was saying, but she was whispering and singing to him softly to keep him quiet and still.

I cautiously made my way to the couch and asked, "Is it okay if I sit down here?" My protecting officer remained standing at the front doorway, seemingly invisible to Nunes. His eyes were focused only on me, which made me both nervous and calm at the same time.

He nodded and motioned towards the couch for me to sit, and he took a seat in the reclining chair across from me. With his head down, he said, "There's no way He'd ever forgive me, sir... I have too much hate in my heart! I'm in agony every day. I hate everything... every breath I take..."

I did my best to try and keep eye contact with him to show my attentiveness and to express compassion and understanding. "Corporal Nunes... or Robert? May I call you Robert?" Without waiting for an answer, I continued, "If you are in agony, there is a solution for that. There is healing. There is a cure. There is hope! ...but only if you are willing to seek that help."

He shook his head and squinted his eyes at me—a sudden wave of rage engulfed his face and I, for the first time, fully grasped the danger that we all were now in. I realized I had to find a way to free his wife and son. I slowly stood and took two steps towards him.

"Robert," I said gently, "I cannot imagine what you went through, saw, and heard in the Middle East, but I know whatever happened over there, you did it for your family... That hope I spoke of can be redeemed today, if you let your wife and son go..."

Unsure of whether I should continue, I assessed his facial features once more. He seemed to be relaxing a bit, even though his eyes continued to dart back and forth, as if he was viewing some invisible movie in fast forward.

Choosing my words carefully, I prayed to speak the right ones. "There was no hope over there. But there is here. You're home now. You can still make the right choice here today. Please, Robert, let your family go. God will account for that. Then, you and I can take the time to sort this whole situation out together. Please, Robert."

Having never had any experience in pleading for a human life before, I wasn't sure how my words would be received.

He looked towards his wife and son, with deep sadness in his eyes, he said to her: "Jennifer, take Henry and just go."

My protective officer at the door opened it quickly, and two other officers rushed in to assist Ms. Nunes and the boy. Within 5 seconds, they had cleared the house.

Feeling momentarily relieved, I knew I needed to express my gratitude. "Thank you, Robert. That was the right decision. You did good."

Robert nodded to himself without looking directly at me, and he stood up and began pacing again.

"Okay, Robert, okay." I was normally someone who spoke a great deal with my hands, but I was trying very hard to be conscious of any sudden or large movements. "Now, Robert, if you're mad at God, that is understandable. It's normal to be upset or angry with Him sometimes. Maybe we could talk about that?" I felt inclined to ask, "Do you think it's possible that while we chat... you could please put your gun down?"

I awaited his response. With his back to me, he began to sob again. I knew I wasn't dealing with just Robert anymore, but various other voices in his head as well. My arm hairs rose with goosebumps, and I contemplated whether I should let him have some time to think or if I should continue speaking. The silence was unbearable, so I chose the latter.

"I, too, have been angry at God before. We all have the right to choose how we feel. That's a privilege He has given us—the choice to love Him and to receive the gift of His love in return."

He didn't respond, his back still to me. He took a deep breath, though, and stopped weeping, his shoulders shaking with the remaining shudders of his hard crying.

I stood and took a slow, gentle step towards him, keeping my voice soft and calm. "Robert, you are not alone. I am here, and God is here with us. He wants you to let go of the anger and hatred in your heart... to see that there is still hope and that He has a plan and a purpose for your life, even if you can't understand what that is right now. Let me help you to make the choice today to choose love..."

Robert turned around, and our eyes met. I was confused by the relaxed, blank expression on his face. He reached out his hand to me. I took it in my own, and holding onto it tightly, he said, "Thank you, chaplain."

He shook my hand and gave me a small smile. He blinked twice, and very softly, almost in a whisper, said, "I don't want to choose love." His smile faded...

I heard the loud "POP!" before my mind could comprehend the fact that he had just lifted his gun to his temple and pulled the trigger.

My face was wet. *Was it raining? No, wait, I was still inside.* My mind swirled. I wiped the wetness from my face only to realize it was red... bright red... blood. It was blood that had splattered. I looked down and I was covered in it. *Dear God! What just happened?*

The whole room began to spin as my body began to quiver. My knees buckled just as I felt the tug of the security officer behind me, forcibly pulling me, guiding me back outside. My last memory of that room would forever be the rapidly expanding pool of blood, seeping into the beige carpet.

The next thing that my mind grasped onto was a shrieking, wailing sound: Mrs. Nunes. Her cries rang in my ears and seemed to echo in my brain.

"Are you alright Chaplain?" asked Deputy Fresno. I nodded untruthfully as he continued, "Chaplain, you did well, sir. You really did the best that you could. You hear me? You did the best that you could. Please, come sit in my vehicle, while we get everything here sorted out and get you back home to your family, okay?" I just kept nodding at everything he was saying to me. My eyes wandered to the clock on the dashboard of his car: 10:07pm.

Confused, I mumbled to no one in particular, "15 minutes...? How...? Only...? Just 15 minutes...?" It all seemed to happen in the blink of an eye... or two... that's all it took—from here, gone to eternity. I could not believe that everything had happened so quickly. 15 minutes had felt like hours.

Deputy Fresno was looking at me strangely, so I simply said, "Okay." I said it to appease him and mislead him to believe I was alright. *Okay... such a strange word. It had been used quite a lot this evening... and nothing about what had happened here was remotely even a tiny bit okay.*

I began to think of what I could have said to prevent the night's incident. I asked the deputy to see his file again. I skimmed over his record until I found his tours and his job description, medals, and EPR's.

He had arrived back to the States 3 weeks ago, was diagnosed 2 weeks ago, and was on waiting list to see mental health specialist. Appointment in 4 weeks?! 4 weeks to see a specialist... that was plenty of time for the disease to grow and consume anyone. We had to do better than that for our men returning home. We just had to.

Deputy Fresno handed me a clipboard and told me to sign the witness form as well as a nondisclosure statement of confidentiality. I didn't question it. I numbly signed my name on the form he handed me and many more that night.

I would have signed anything. I was there. I had seen it. I had been the last person to speak to Corporal Nunes. *Had I done my best? What should I have said differently? Was this my fault? Why did this happen? What was the point...? What was the point...?* Nunes' voice echoed in my mind. The questions were spinning, bouncing, twisting... The only thing I knew for certain was that Corporal Nunes' blood was on my hands... figuratively and literally...

CHAPTER 7
~ Finding the Way Back Home ~

Jordan

The shock was beginning to wear off a bit. I needed to take a few more deep breaths before I drove myself home. I decided to check my phone. I had 4 missed calls: Chaplain Dubose, Joanna (twice), and Sergeant Miller. So, I decided to call within the chain of command. I spoke briefly with Joanna and told her that I was okay and that I would be home within an hour.

Next, I called Chaplain Dubose to brief him on the night's events. He repeated his remorse and was apologetic, and he said to take off as much time as I needed. He would cover my hours. He also said he'd call Sergeant Miller for me.

Time had been a roller coaster for the last few days. The days were going by so slowly; my nights were so quick to dissolve. It was like a magician had been playing a dirty trick on me the whole time.

As I drove toward my house, I began to pray and ask God for understanding... and forgiveness. I began to cry, then weep. I parked outside the garage and decided to let all my emotions out until I had nothing left—heaving so hard my face, my head, began to throb. I calmed down after about twenty seconds and became instantly cognizant that I needed the comfort of my Joanna.

I turned off the engine and routinely slid the keys into my pocket as I got out of the car and closed the door, with a loud bang that startled me for a moment. I took a deep, shuddering breath and numbly walked towards my front door. Before I even placed my hand on the knob, it was opened.

Joanna threw herself on me with a loving and comforting embrace, having been awaiting my arrival. I begin to cry again and unload my grief. She was my best friend, and the only person that truly understood me. Without even talking, she began to weep with me also. After a few minutes, she kissed me on the cheek. Her loving hand consoled me with a circular gesture on my back and affirmed how much she loved me.

She closed the door behind me, grabbed my hand, and walked me down the hall towards our room, like a young child being guided to his room for bedtime. I closed our door and begin to discourse without encrypting details.

*****

The next morning, I woke up to find Joanna out of bed. I got up and did my morning ritual; brushed my teeth, shaved, showered, and groomed—took a total of about 30 minutes.

As I opened my bedroom door, I could smell the aroma of a delicious breakfast waiting for me—coffee, bacon, pancakes, maple syrup... I sure needed it, since I didn't sleep much last night. Joanna saw me and instantly stopped what she was doing to come give me a hug and a kiss.

"Good morning, sweetheart. I love you." I felt the sincerity in her voice.

I answered back, "I love you, too, honey. Thank you. It smells great in here."

As we ate breakfast, Joanna told me that Chaplain Dubose had texted her earlier that morning to ask how I was doing, to see if I needed anything, and to tell me that if I needed to that I should stay home from work today.

Emotionally, I felt fine, or at least I thought I did. Mentally and physically, I was drained. I woke up without guilt. However, I was still confused as to how and why it had happened, and my heart was filled with sorrow for the now widow and her son.

I asked Joanna what she had told the girls about what happened, and she said, "I told them Daddy had an emergency last night, and he's sleeping in, so please be very quiet. They're fine, darling. As long as you're alright, they'll have a good day."

I decided to go to work just for an hour or so, in order to speak with Dubose around lunch. As I pulled up, I parked in the visitor space instead of my reserved spot. I took a deep breath and hoped I didn't run into anybody.

As I opened the back door, I could hear people talking amongst themselves in their offices, so I decided to speed walk towards Dubose's office. I could see his door open.

As I approached, I knocked, and he looked up from his computer. He immediately stopped what he was doing, got up, and softly said, "Oh, Jordan..." He walked up to me, opened his arms, and hugged me tightly. "I'm just so sorry..."

My initial thought was, *Yeah, right. You're sorry for what happened, or you're sorry for the pathetic excuse you made that got me into all of this...* However, I brushed off that blunt, ruthless notion, cleared my personal thoughts, and decided to forgive him because that's what Jesus would do. I was going to do my best to appreciate his earnestness.

I closed his door, and he pointed for me to sit down on his couch. Then, he chose to sit next to me rather than in front of me. He began by apologizing for not taking the call last night and asking for my forgiveness, which did actually soften my heart a bit. He then asked me how I was doing and if there was anything he or the staff could do for me. It turned out to be a nicer conversation than I was expecting.

As we were wrapping things up, he placed his hand on my shoulder and interjected, "Oh, by the way, Jordan, Ms. Nunes, the wife, has been calling here nonstop all morning asking for you. She direly wishes to speak with you about last night."

I tried not to react in any way as he continued, "I told her I'd let her know when you're available to talk, which I understand may be some time. Also, I'm taking this Sunday (preaching) from you. Go rest, and don't worry about coming in Monday and Tuesday either. Please, just enjoy the whole Thanksgiving week off with your family."

I didn't really know what to say, so I simply nodded and said, "Thank you, sir."

I stood up and gave him a handshake that mildly transitioned into a half hug. I walked out his doorway and headed to my office, very quietly, incognito. I slowly opened my door and closed it, leaving the lights off to ensure my presence would go unnoticed. I just needed to check a few things on my computer, and then I was going to take his advice and head home. I really didn't want to be anywhere but with my family.

CHAPTER 8
~ Thanksgiving's Acquiescence ~

Jordan

Saturday morning, two days after the terrible incident, I was still struggling with a way to absolve the images and sequence of events out of my head. I decided that I was going to do my best to unwind.

Lily would be up any minute, and I was looking forward to her innocence that could detox the treacherous mental images that were playing like a continuous slideshow in my brain. Becca wouldn't be up for hours—a typical teenager. Lord help us all if we were to wake her up.

I did feel the urge to help Joanna clean the house, but I decided that it was probably best to stay out of her way until I was a bit more up to speed. She was a sanitizing whirlwind since my mother was coming into town for Thanksgiving.

My mother wasn't perfect, but she had done what she could when we were growing up. She did her best, as a single mother, to raise 3 children, all on her own. My struggles couldn't compare to her circumstances, and for that, I was thankful that God had been graceful to me, allowing me to show love and grace in return to my mother.

She was a tough cookie, who spoke her mind, quite boldly and bluntly, but she was also very compassionate. I was looking forward to her arrival, and I was hopeful that she'd cook one of her signature dishes. Cooking always made her feel happy and useful, and Joanna was happy to not have to cook. The girls, too, were pleased when Grandma came to get to try something new.

My mother had me at the age of 16, just a teenager. How in the world was she able to? Becca was merely 15 and still couldn't quite figure out how to put on her bra correctly some days.

My childhood had been rough—one of poverty, hunger, lack of shelter, and watching my mother go from one abusive relationship to another. I could not fault her for my past. Now, having been through all that, I was filled with love and gratitude towards her. Because of all the pain we (my siblings and I) suffered, I was able to find solace and healing in God.

Despite being a single mother and all the challenges she had faced, she really did try. *A single mother... I knew someone who just recently became one...*

The clanking sound of Joanna taking pots and pans out of the kitchen cabinet downstairs snapped me out of my heavy thoughts. I decided to wander down to the kitchen, and there I found Joanna making breakfast. Perhaps helping her would keep my mind busy and would help it not to dwell on those horrendous thoughts zooming through my mind.

Pretending to act as if nothing happened, so close, so intimately, was inconceivable. I shook away my thoughts and decided sternly to focus on my family—for my will had to be greater than carnal lapse.

*****

Sunday rolled around, and I made the decision to read over my notes from the already prepared sermon that I would have talked about this morning: "The Power of Prayer". My heart struck a chord as I read the verse that I had chosen to focus on, James 5:16: "Therefore, confess your sins to one another and pray for one another, that you may be healed. The prayer of a righteous person has great power as it is working."

How God handled this, I did not know, but it affirmed my conviction on what I needed to do: speak with and pray for the Widow Nunes.

I had been so selfish, praying for my own thoughts to be freed from the trauma of that awful night that I had forgotten who had been affected even more. My selfishness had been letting me drown in uncertainty and guilt, from which I so desperately wanted to be free. This verse reminded me that, most importantly, we all needed to find healing.

I closed my notes and hollered to Joanna, "We're going to the chapel!

*****

As we headed to church, I ran through my thoughts of what I would say if I happened to see Ms. Nunes there.

"Jordan, do you want to sit in the back this time? I know you don't want people hovering, asking questions," Joanna asked, concerned.

"Well, I don't want to seem like I'm hiding either, so let's see if we can sit in the middle," I replied, as we parked and exited the car.

The girls were surprisingly behaving like heavenly angels. I wondered what kind of bribe Joanna had negotiated with them in order to keep them this tranquil and mannerly. I kissed them both and told them that I loved them. I had made a mental note to make more of an effort to do that more often.

As we opened the door to enter the chapel, we automatically started shaking hands and greeting the members of the congregation, as if nothing eventful had happened. Astonishingly, it seemed that not a lot of people knew of the incident that had just occurred three days ago. No one mentioned it, or perhaps they were being courteous and considerate...? When people had asked why I wasn't preaching, all I could respond was that I needed to rest.

Jim and George, our parish ushers, rushed over to me and asked if I'd like to be escorted to the front. I quickly shook my head and said to them as nonchalantly as I could manage, "Thank you, Jim, George. I will be sitting with my family today..."

They both smiled, as I asked, "How are you gentlemen doing this morning?"

They each, in their own turn, acknowledged, while nodding their heads, that they were both doing well. I shook their hands and then continued to walk with Joanna and the girls towards the middle of the chapel.

Finding an almost empty pew, we sat down in the space available and settled right in. There was a lady sitting next to me, but I didn't look too carefully at who, not wanting to strike up a conversation with anyone unnecessarily. However, before I knew it, I felt a tap on my shoulder, and she spoke softly, "Chaplain Ramonda, how are you?"

I turned my head to answer, and I realized that I had been seated next to Miss Blanca Wade. I smiled and responded, "I'm well, Miss Blanca. Thank you for asking. How are you today?"

She smiled and said, "Good. God will restore me in due season, but in the meantime, it is well with my soul."

I smiled back at her. "Amen. Glad to hear you're holding onto that faith. He will restore you."

Miss Blanca had been a faithful attendee and helpful volunteer with the chapel. She hadn't formally come in to my office to discuss her personal life, but from what she had told Joanna, she had one grown adult child who was in the military, and when she talked about him, she would become uneased. Joanna did say more about her, but I didn't have much of a recollection of what it was. I'm pretty sure she told me while I was watching football.

By some means, I felt peace, sitting as a congregational member rather than the preacher. It was nice to participate in the praise and worship, rather than lead it. It also could be my wife; she was the soothing aloe to all my pain and wounds.

As I looked over to her, her head bowed down, her long, dark eyelashes rested on her porcelain cheeks. I smiled with a sigh of relief, thanking God for her and my two beautiful girls. She had been my helpmate, protecting and teaching me. I found it astonishing how God sent angels in many different forms, but I could safely claim my wife was Heaven sent.

As I tried to become more attentive to the praise and worship, I felt another tap on my shoulder. It was Sergeant Miller. He whispered in my ear, "Sir, I wasn't sure if you were coming today, but seeing as you're here, just wanted to let you know Ms. Jennifer Nunes is here, and she has been hoping to talk to you. I just wanted to let you know so that you won't feel bombarded after the service."

I nodded and whispered, "Thank you."

He walked away, and I turned to an already curious Joanna. "She's here. Ms. Nunes is here. I'll be going to my office after the service. Please take the girls out to eat for lunch and come back and pick me up."

She nodded once and continued to worship. I decided to turn around, get on my knees, and pray for wisdom as to what to say to her when she approached me. As worship ended and Chaplain Dubose neared the pulpit to begin, I ended my prayer, sat back in the pew, and committed to doing my best to not be distracted and listen to the message.

God knows all things, and there are no coincidences. I couldn't help but smile, as Chaplain Dubose opened his Bible and began reading his message's focus verse: James 5:16.

*****

As Chaplain Dubose wrapped up God's message, which was very much directed at me, we all were asked to stand for the final prayer. My heart began to pound nervously, because I knew the time to speak with Ms. Nunes was drawing near. I refused to crane my neck around and look for her. I knew the confrontation was coming, which was both a blessing and a curse. I prayed extra hard as Joanna squeezed my hand, sensing my nervousness.

As Chaplain Dubose closed his prayer and with a hearty, echoed "Amen" from the congregation, Joanna and I looked at each other. She leaned on me to kiss me reassuringly on the cheek, turned around towards the girls, and quickly told them it was time to go have lunch "just the girls", giving them a look not to ask and that she would explain in a few minutes.

As I walked through the pews, a few people stopped to greet me and ask questions. It took a while, but I had finally made it almost to my office, when I heard a woman's voice calling my name, "Chaplain Ramonda!" I proceeded into my office, pretending that I had not heard her. I needed a moment to take a deep breath. I hurriedly sat down at my desk and looked towards the doorway, anticipating Ms. Nunes' arrival.

As I heard her approach the door, I did my best to look calm and kind. However, it was Miss Blanca that appeared in the doorway. I mentally sighed in relief as she entered and announced, "Sir, I just wanted to let you know I'm available in advance for the Christmas party if you need any volunteers."

Because I knew I wasn't going to remember, I countered, "Thank you, Miss Blanca. That's very noble of you. Listen, please do me a favor and tell Sergeant Miller so that he can write it down for me...?

"Say no more! Of course! Have a Happy Sunday and Happy Thanksgiving!" She used my signature trademark.

Once she had left my office, I turned on my computer and looked over a few things, while I opened my bottle of water. Just like her situation had been that night—startling—she was at my office door.

Without knocking, she stepped into my office and said, "Chaplain?"

I swallowed my gulp of water quickly, hoping not to choke. "Yes, ma'am?"

"My name is Jennifer Nunes, and I believe we were not formally introduced the other night. I've been eagerly trying to get a hold of you..."

I responded, "Yes, yes, I heard. Ms. Nu—Jennifer. May I call you Jennifer? Please, have a seat."

She sat down on the couch, put her purse on the floor, and without hesitation, put her hands over her face and sobbed. That couch had a tendency to do that.

After a minute or so, she composed herself. "Sir, I just wanted to say thank you!" She inhaled very hard, while her tears streamed down her face. "Thank you so much! You saved me and my son, Henry!"

I handed her the tissue box next to me. "Jennifer, I am so sorry for your loss. Thank you for coming in to see me." ...and I really meant that. I had been so focused grief, guilt, and on losing Robert that I hadn't thought much to be grateful for Ms. Nunes and her son being saved.

I did my best to give her sincere reassurance. "Please know that you have a team of chaplains here if you or your son need any of our assistance, besides the resources provided to you from the FRC (Family Readiness Center) and mental health facility." I paused then, wondering how helpful that seemed to her. Having read Robert's file over and over again, I had read that they had already put in a request for a mental health and wellness appointment, but that the soonest they were able to be seen was one month out.

I leaned forward and earnestly said, "I wish I could have helped Robert more, and I'll never know if I could have—"

She interrupted, "You couldn't have! He was suffering, and he didn't want to be a burden on me or on Henry anymore. I loved Robert before the war..." She paused, momentarily lost in thought. "I know I made a vow to love him in sickness and in health, but that wasn't Robert who came back." She shook her head trying to rid her mind of the images that threatened to overtake it.

"As harsh as this sounds, you saved and liberated us from a monster who tortured us... and for that, I just wanted to thank you." She sighed softly as she stood up. "I'm not sure how I will explain this all to my 3-year-old... but I plan to leave tomorrow and be with my family for Thanksgiving and for a couple of weeks after."

I responded poignantly, "Absolutely, that's probably best for now. Please, remember if you need anything, like I said, feel free to call me or anyone here at the chapel."

She picked up her purse, and as she wrapped it around her shoulder she said, "Thank you, Chaplain. I will. I'm so sorry you had to see that... I pray God gives you strength, as well, to continue your calling and His plan for your life. I know I couldn't do this as a vocation or career."

She smiled warmly as she took my hand in both of hers. "Okay, then, I'm not going to take up any more of your time. I saw you with your family earlier. I just wanted to thank you sincerely..." She made sure to make direct eye contact as she added with emphasis, "Thank you for saving us."

As she strode out the door, I sat back down at my desk. I, too, felt relieved having spoken with her. I was grateful that she wasn't resenting me in any way for her husband's death. I took a deep breath, rubbed my face with both hands, and shut down my computer.

I looked at my watch and realized all that just took 10 minutes (including Ms. Blanca!). I reached for my cellphone and decided to call Joanna to let her know that I would just eat something at home, but she let me know, sounding pleased, "Honey, we never left. We're here in the parking lot waiting for you. Just in case you weren't going to be very long, we decided to wait for you for a bit."

"Excellent! I'll be right there!" I turned the lights off in my office and rushed out. I gave a quick nod to Sergeant Miller, and he responded with a thumbs up, indicating that it was no problem, and he would lock up.

Sergeant Miller really was a wonderful assistant—if only he knew how much of big help he was by being faithful in the little things. He was our support system. I needed to make sure that he knew that next time I saw him. I always wanted to make sure my support system was well taken care of.

I stepped outside and saw Joanna parked out in the back. As I walked towards them, she got out and walked over to the passenger side so that I could drive.

As I got into the car, Joanna reminded me that we needed to go to the commissary afterwards and go grocery shopping for Thanksgiving week. I smiled. That actually sounded like fun. I was happy to be with my family.

Having spoken to Ms. Nunes, it felt like the weight had been lifted from my shoulders. It was going to be a good week. I just knew it.

CHAPTER 9
~ A Different Light ~

Jordan

Ah, Monday... how I don't despise you this day! I usually embraced any day that I had off. I sure hoped that this week would go by slowly. Uninterrupted "Quadruple F" satisfaction was every man's wish: spending the holidays with Family, Friends, Food, and, last but not least, Football!

That being said, I still had to help clean up around the house and do my assigned "manly" chores before I headed out to pick up my mother from the airport. Today, my "honey-do" list consisted of mowing the lawn, taking out the trash, vacuuming, and whatever else the boss asked me to do. I couldn't complain. Joanna always did so much around the house, so I was thankful to have time to help her out. Plus, this year's list was considerably smaller than last year's. Ha!

I think that was mainly because Becca, now 15, had more responsibilities. I no longer had to clean our vehicles! I should have a pretty relaxing week—no work, no on-call, no studying, no... nothing.

As I finished all my chores, I quickly went inside to have lunch with the girls.

After quickly eating a turkey and Swiss sandwich with some potato chips on the side, I asked Joanna, "Honey, I'm going to take a quick shower, okay?"

She nodded, and I ruffled Lily's hair a bit as I left the kitchen. As I started up the stairs, I could hear her say, "Daddy is silly today..." And, I smiled.

Getting into the shower, the water drizzled all over my body, and I felt myself relax. The hot shower cleansed me from sweat, grass residue, gasoline smell, and outdoor stench...

"Jordan!" I heard Joanna yelling from the kitchen, and I didn't know why because we've established a million times that one could not be heard fully from our bathroom.

"Jordan!" This time her voice was louder as she was nearing the bathroom. I rushed to wash the shampoo out of my hair, turned off the water, and grabbed a towel, just as she burst through the bathroom door.

"Jordan! It's the Dallas TSA calling. Your mother fainted during the flight and is being taken to the hospital. Here's the EMT on the phone for you."

I hastily took the phone from Joanna. "Hello, this is Jordan, Miriam's son." I took a deep breath and exhaled.

The EMT responded, "Yes, hello, sir. Your mother is conscious for now. We're taking her to Becker Hospital to get evaluated. Her blood pressure is a bit high, and we suspect her blood sugar may be low. We will further test her once we arrive at the hospital. She showed us all her medication, and from seeing the variations she has, most likely she will spend the night for evaluation." He paused a moment, and I could hear some shuffling going on in the background. "Are you still there, sir?" he asked.

I nodded, trying to process everything he was saying. Then, I realized he needed verbal confirmation. "Yes, yes... I'm still here."

"Alright. She's currently receiving oxygen, so I can't put her on the phone right now. I'll give your information to the nurse as soon as we arrive at the hospital, and they will call your cellphone when she gets admitted."

"Yes, okay, thank you, sir. I'll head to the hospital right now." I hung up the phone and looked towards Joanna. I could tell that she was trying to remain calm, but she was fidgeting with her hands, like she always did when she was nervous.

"Joanna, I have to go, it will be alright." I tried to sound reassuring and confident. "I'll call you on my way there, and when I get there" She nodded and moved out of my way so that I could get dressed.

I militarily put my clothes on in under sixty seconds. I could feel my day sinking into the abyss with no way up the surface. I fought the negativity and said a quick prayer for my mother and for peace in my heart.

Joanna intercepted my thoughts, "Honey, do you want us to go with you?"

I shook my head. "No, honey, they're just doing tests for now, and they will keep her overnight. Just pray she'll get released tomorrow, that it isn't anything serious, and that we'll be on our way back home quickly."

Dallas was a 4-hour drive away, which I despised. However, I did take note to be thankful that this hadn't happened in Philadelphia, where she had originally departed. Well, it wasn't how I imagined my Thanksgiving week beginning, but when it rained, it sure did pour.

As I made my way to the front door, I kissed the girls and hugged Joanna tightly. I got in my car, said another quick prayer for safety, and began to pull out of the driveway. I looked up at the house one last time to see Joanna waving her hands like a crazy person. I stopped and rolled down my window.

She ran to the car's side, her face flushed from hurrying. "Here, honey, I almost forgot. I wrapped you a couple of sandwiches so that you have something to eat on your way."

I grabbed her hand and pulled her inward. After giving her a big kiss, I grasped her face with both my hands, and looking at her with an ardent stare, I said intently, "I love you... so much."

She smiled broadly and pushed herself back away from the car. "I love you too. Be safe."

*****

I called Joanna within the hour after I had left and asked her to call my sister and update her on the situation. My sister never handled situations like this well, and I really didn't feel like speaking with her right now, since she was melodramatic and would probably freak out.

As soon as I hung up with Joanna, my phone rang; it was a Dallas area code. I immediately picked it up.

"Mr. Ramonda?" the woman's voice on the other side of the line asked.

I responded, "Yes, ma'am?"

"Hi, this is Marty, the head nurse, on the 4th floor, where your mother was just admitted about half an hour ago. We were trying to get her to talk to us and give us as much information as possible, but it seemed that she was struggling to breathe, so we sedated her to calm her nerves."

"Okay, thank you for letting me know. I'm on my way up there. I have about 3 hours to go. Is there anything I should bring?"

She answered, "Not at this moment, sir. She showed us her medication that she had with her, but we need her whole medication list. If there's any way you could provide us with that information to help the doctors, that would be great."

I paused momentarily and thought about the easiest way to accomplish that. "Okay, I'll have to call my sister who cares for her, and I'll make sure that information gets to you."

"Perfect! Thank you, sir. When you get here, be sure to park in the long-term parking lot; it's cheaper. Also, she's staying in room 401C. If you have any questions, feel free to call back at this number and ask for the 4th floor head nurse. Again, my name is Marty."

I thought she was going to hang up then, but she quickly added, "Oh, and if you'd like to speak with your mother, dial the room number as the extension... but I'd wait an hour or so till the drugs wear off and she's fully conscious."

I cleared my throat and said, "Okay, thank you, Ms. Marty. I appreciate your care. Call me if anything else important occurs before I get there."

"Yes, sir! I sure will. See you soon."

After hanging up, I immediately called Joanna to reiterate everything that I just heard and asked her to please call my sister for all the requested information and then have her contact the nurse herself. My wife, my partner, my other half—she was always on top of things. I appreciated it greatly when she helped me like this. I wished I could give her the moon and more. Her selfless character and willing servitude were the definition of what Christianity is.

Earlier when I first called her, I was ranting a bit about how one thing piles on top of another and how I just wished to have a peaceful, tranquil week without any interruptions. She astutely responded with reason and helped me to see things from a more positive perspective.

"You have to be thankful you are free today to take care of your mother, honey. God will never give you more than you can handle."

She let that sink in for moment. "Think about it. If your boss had taken that suicidal incident, he'd be off this week, while you had to go to work. You'd have to stay here and be on-call instead, and you'd be worried about your mom."

True. She was right. She often could help me see these events in a better, different light. I resolved to try and think positively. I turned on the radio to worship music and was going to make the most of the next few hours of my drive to meditate and spend some quality time with God.

CHAPTER 10
~ Answered Prayers ~

<u>Jordan</u>

As I arrived at the hospital, I parked in the long-term parking lot, taking Marty's advice. It sure was a long walk, though. I strode inside patient care. The customer service desk was right in the front, but there was no one seated there behind the counter. I surveyed the area until I found the hospital map to try and figure out where to go on my own. Down the short hallway on the right, take a left, elevator to the right to the 4th floor. Got it.

As I got in the elevator, I prayed that my mother was alright. So far, I wasn't terribly concerned. She frequently had something going on with her physically... "My foot is broken..." "My shoulder is dislocated..." "My hip is bruised..." My mother was a master at hyperboles, and at times, I couldn't decipher what was fact or fantasy in her mind.

The elevator stopped and opened to the 4th floor. As I exited, I looked around to find the main desk. I followed the signs on the wall that led to room 401C. Finishing down a long hallway, I turned left, and from there, I could see room 401C. Her name ("Miriam Sanders") was there on a file on the door.

I knocked and heard a soft voice say, "Come on in" I pushed the door open to see my mother awake, sitting up, and watching TV while eating her Jell-O. She smiled as I walked in; she looked pretty good, to be honest.

I grinned. "Making trouble already, Mom?"

She laughed. "You know it!"

I was relieved to see her looking well, so I asked her, "Are you alright?"

She scooted up on her bed and got comfortable to talk to me, while I sat on the patient chair next to her. "Yeah, just fine. My blood pressure was high, and I think I may have mixed up one of my medicines. That, plus the altitude, I guess I just collapsed."

"Have they done all the tests needed to be done?"

She answered, "Yes, they have one more in a couple of hours, and they said if all goes well, we can go home tomorrow morning. So sorry, son. Could you call the airline and book us a flight?"

I chuckled. "Mom, we're only 4 hours away. I drove up here. By the way, Joanna and the girls say 'hello' and are excited to see you."

We talked and chatted away for the next hour or so. I decided it was time to get comfortable in the patient chair next to my mother, since I knew I would have to sleep there for the night.

One of the nurses came in and said that it was time to do the last test and asked if I could step outside for a few minutes. I nodded and assured my mom I'd be back as soon as I got some food and coffee. After I approached the snack bar, purchased a hot dog and bag of chips, and walked back to the 4th floor waiting room, I took out my cellphone to call Joanna.

As I began to dial her number, I heard someone sniffling behind me. I nonchalantly turned around and saw a woman about my mother's age crying and blowing her nose. I put my phone away and ate the last few bites of my hot dog.

God tugged at my heart, and I knew I needed to speak with the woman. It made it a bit easier to start up a conversation, seeing as how we were the only two people in the waiting room.

I got up and walked towards the lady to sit across from her. I did my best to smiley kindly, and I asked, "Family member?"

She nodded, "Yes, my mother. She's 77 and having heart surgery tomorrow with a 20% chance of survival." She cried softly. "I just got back here to the waiting room from kissing her goodnight and possibly not seeing her tomorrow alive."

With caution and with respect, I said. "I am sorry to hear that. Are you here by yourself?"

"Yes, my father passed away 2 years ago, my brother passed away at a young age from cancer, as well, and my sister is in Alaska unable to make it. My husband went to our house to feed the dogs, and I told him to stay and spend the night at home while I stayed here."

I slowly nodded. "I see. What's your name? Your mother's?"

She answered, "I'm Linda, and my mother is Margaret."

"Linda, if you'd allow me, I'd love to pray for you and your mother. Would that be okay?

She nodded and began to cry harder. I took her hand, bowed my head, and begin to pray this prayer:

"Dear Lord, Linda and I come before you as humble servants to lift up Margaret. Lord, we ask that You guide the doctor's hands during this surgery and for him to be attentive, careful, and precise and to have a successful operation. Heavenly Father, we ask for supernatural protection, intervention, and healing for Margaret. Although science says that there is only a 20% chance of survival, with You here with us we know that there is a 100% chance. If that is your will Lord, let it be done. Father, I pray for Linda to have the strength, patience, and peace with tomorrow's outcome. Console her anxiety, embrace her, and show her Your love throughout this process. We ask all this in the name of Jesus. Amen."

I opened my eyes and watched her take a big sigh of relief. I offered her some coffee, but she declined. She said she felt better and decided to go home to her husband. We talked for a few more minutes about where she was from, why I was there, and so on. I didn't discuss much about my mother being here, since I was slightly embarrassed that this woman was about the very same age as my mom, and her mother was here for a severe medical reason, as opposed to mine being here for clumsiness. As she got up to leave, I looked at my watch. It was almost 8pm, so I finally called Joanna.

"Hi, honey I'm here at the hospital…" I updated her on my mother's condition and status. I began to grumble about my mom and how I had to drive 4 hours and waste gas, all because my mom was irresponsible and didn't take her medicine properly. I also told her about having just met Linda, about Margaret, and their whole situation…

As I finished speaking, I heard her chuckle in the background. "Well, I don't mean to be too optimistic, but didn't you ask God for Him to cleanse your mind? You've been so preoccupied with your mother, have you thought once of the incident that happened here last week?"

She paused to make sure I was still on the line, and then added, "Exactly. He works in mysterious and humorous ways, and regardless of how He answers our prayers, it's ultimately His decision. Besides, Linda needed that prayer, and God allowed you to be there for her when she was in distress."

Joanna was the epitome of the reasons why God created women, and I could see it more every day. Joanna was a remarkable woman; she was made for me. A preacher's wife is an ordinary woman in an extraordinary role. She was looked upon as a spiritual leader, whether she wanted that role or not, simply because she was married to a Christian pastor.

When making a vow to marry a minister, she entered a vigorous pact with God Himself—that she would be submissive to God's ministry, always support her husband, and live a humanitarian lifestyle—the last of which could help or hurt the marriage, depending on if both parties agreed.

There was no retirement in God's ministry, for it was continuously about working hard, supporting one another, growing as one, and exercising love, which endured pain, suffering, misunderstandings, hardships, and everything else that entailed.

Although Moses was chosen to lead the people out of Egypt, he was adamant about having Aaron to help him elaborate and execute God's will to be done. At times, that sentiment could be applied to pastors. Sometimes, we couldn't connect well with our sheep, but the soft, dainty voice of a Godly woman could get through without any problems.

A majority of aircraft transportation required two pilots to take off, fly, and land upon the desired destination. There was always the lead pilot and, oftentimes, the co-pilot. The lead pilot oversaw the journey, the mission, and the major important mechanisms of the aircraft itself; while the co-pilot followed the lead of the pilot and handled the minor stuff to ensure a decent takeoff, smooth travel, and safe landing.

The pronouns were ultimately the co-pilot's duty, and the verbs were the pilot's. The lead pilot would be held accountable for the incomplete or completed assignment, but that was why it was important to have the co-pilot's help and support. In the end, they were both essential for the completion of the mission.

I knew that Joanna would be the best co-pilot ever when I met her. She helped me, watched over me, and could take over if she needed—like the strong Queen Esther. Queen Esther was always respectful and submissive. However, she stood up and spoke up when she needed to, for God's plan, because the king was oblivious to what was going on around him. She helped him see the scheme behind an evil agenda.

Kings (and often men, in general) are oblivious to things sometimes—slow to catch on, slow to understand, and (most of the time) insensitive. For a king to lead the country, the queen must first handle her domestic role and lead her palace.

I always had peace knowing that the girls were taken care of, cooked for, taken to the doctor, etc. It reassured me and gave me peace of mind that our home was alright, while I protected them from harm's way outside of our home.

As time and time had proven, my wife had a different kind of strength that I didn't have. During the upcoming holidays, I was particularly thankful for her. Maybe God wanted me to appreciate this Thanksgiving for His works, rather than my enthusiasm for football.

I finished up my phone call with Joanna, but before we ended the call, I said a quick "I love you" to Lily and Becca.

After I hung up, I closed my eyes and rested my head back with a huge sigh. I was tired, exhausted, and cold—I had forgotten how cold hospitals could be. It could be overwhelming at a hospital sometimes—death always just waiting for someone right around the corner, eager to take his next victim.

As chaplains, we either prayed to fight death or let it take the body of the person, as we were there to console and pray for the souls of the loved ones left behind. In either case, hospitals contained a broad range of emotions at any time, and they often could be both exhausting and overwhelming.

I decided to head back to my mother's room to see how she was doing, and as I was about to open the door, the nurse peeked her head out signaled for me to wait in the hallway for just a moment.

"Mr. Ramonda," she began, "your mom is doing fine. She is asleep now from all the commotion and testing. She will have one more test at 6am in the morning, and then after that, she should be able to go home, around a 7am discharge." She smiled, pleased with the news she was sharing with me.

I responded, "Thank you, ma'am. I'm relieved to hear that. Do you have any suggestions or accommodations that I need to adjust for my mom in the next few days?"

She chuckled. "Well, monitor her for the next 2-3 days to make sure that she's taking her medicine correctly and at the right time. As for Thanksgiving, make sure she doesn't eat too many sweets..." She paused for a minute and tried to remember. "Oh, and no alcohol, of course!"

I smiled. "Ok, that all can be done."

She patted my shoulder reassuringly, as I passed her to enter my mother's room, and she added, "I opened the sleeping chair for you and brought you a pillow and a blanket. In case you need anything, please feel free to come to the nurses' station and ask. My name is Pam, by the way."

"Thank you so much, Pam, for your kindness. I sure will."

Before I even fully entered the room, I could hear the loud snoring of my mother in her deep sleep. *Oh, Lord, please help me get some sleep tonight...*

*****

I woke up due to the beeping of my mother's heart monitor, ringing for the 9th time at every hour. Finally, at 5am, I decided to just get some super strong devil's coffee and breakfast. Four hours of sleep was better than none.

It was Tuesday—my second day off and, yet, no full rest. *Please, God, let me have a fulfilled Thanksgiving—no disruptions or emergencies. Let us drive home today safe and sound.*

I got up, walked to my mom's bathroom, and gargled with some mouthwash the hospital offered me. I washed my face thoroughly and used the bathroom as quietly as I could. I gently opened the door to leave my mother's room and softly closed the door behind me.

I texted Joanna that I was awake, just in case, for some miraculous reason, she was too, and she could call me. She called immediately right back. *That woman.* I smiled broadly.

"Hi, honey, how are you?" she said.

I yawned. "Baby, I didn't mean to wake you up. I just didn't sleep well with all the noise and conditions around me, but so far, we should be set to head out this morning if all goes well at her 6am testing."

Joanna said, "Ah, okay... sounds good. Well, why don't you get some breakfast and coffee and call me later?"

I nodded in response, not really thinking about the fact she couldn't see me. "Yes, I was going to. I'll keep you posted. Love you."

"Love you, too, bye."

I walked towards the cafeteria and looked around for some breakfast and strong coffee. I didn't see anything appealing. There was just something about "eating" a meal at a hospital. Eerie? Unsanitary? I didn't know. So, I only got coffee from the coffee shop.

When I returned to my mom's room, she was awake, looking bright and sunny, and chatting with the nurse. I couldn't quite see the nurse's name tag. Janie? Jamie? I didn't want to awkwardly stare to investigate, so as is standard protocol, I asked with an appropriate generic noun. "Good morning, ma'am. How's my mom doing?"

My mom answered for her. "I'm doing great, dear. I didn't get the best sleep, but I'm sure I'll take advantage of that on the drive to your house."

The nurse turned towards me then. "Good morning, sir. I'm Janet. I'm just doing one last blood pressure test on your mom, but she looks good to go. I just need to submit this for the physician's approval for discharge."

"Okay, awesome."

I stepped outside her room just to let them finish, leaned against the wall, and took a much-needed gulp of my coffee. It tasted awful, but I could tell it was plenty strong, which was really all that mattered to me.

As I looked around, I saw a familiar face standing by the nurse's station. It was Linda, from the waiting room last night. We made eye contact and approached one another. She appeared to be refreshed, with a look of glee on her face.

"Mr. Ramonda! I'm glad to see you! I was hoping to catch you before you left. I didn't know what room your mom was in, but I knew you'd be in this hallway at some point." She snickered.

"Anyways, the doctor called me last night after I got home. You won't believe it! They're postponing the surgery because miraculously her left heart valve began to work, so they're monitoring it now. The surgeon says he's never seen a Lazarus of the heart valve in his career. I asked him, 'Let's say it becomes stable, would she still need surgery?' He said that may still be a possibility, but that the chances of survival were now up to 70%!"

Linda did a happy little jump and continued, "I began to cry out to God and shout out, 'Thank you!' I had been so hopeless, just feeling defeated by this disease."

She reached for my hand and sandwiched mine kindly between both of hers. "I want to thank you for praying for me and my mother and her healing, for a miracle, for my rest and anxiety... all of it. Thank you, thank you, thank you! You must know you were a Godsend."

She turned around and picked up a canister with a bow wrapped around it. "I made you a little something this morning—some Danish sweets, muffins, homemade asiago bagels, and a few more goodies."

I had no words. I felt a sudden drowning of my voice. I was hungry and appreciative. "Thank you, Linda. You didn't have to do that. This looks great. I actually haven't eaten breakfast, so you just blessed me this morning with your thoughtfulness."

I grabbed a napkin that she had on the side and picked out a bagel. "I am so glad your mom is doing better. God hears our prayers, and I firmly believe that."

She choked up a bit, while smiling. "I do now... I had forgotten the power of prayer and want to thank you for restoring my faith in God."

We talked for a few more minutes before I had to let her go, because I saw Nurse Janet exit my mother's room. We parted ways, both satisfied with blessed mornings. She had worked so hard, baking so many goodies. Sometimes, the littlest things could bring joy during times of need.

My mother's discharge papers were all in order, and we began to get ready to pack up and go. I may have been tired, but I was well-fed. Looking on the positive side, I would get to go home and rest, while the girls wore out my mother.

*****

On the drive home, we started to talk about life, work, family... After an hour or so, my mother fell asleep. I sped just a bit—10mph over the speed limit, just to cut half an hour off my drive time.

I called Joanna and updated her on everything that happened that morning. She told me she had everything taken care of for Thanksgiving and not to worry. I gave a sigh of relief; I had been sure I was going to have things to do when arriving back home. But, as usual, my superwoman had resolved it.

After hanging up the phone with Joanna, I put on some light, melodic music to finish the drive. One hour and thirty minutes left...

*****

As we entered our subdivision, I woke up my mother. "Mom, wake up... we're here."

She sat up and yawned. "That was some good rest!"

I giggled. "It's noon, Mom. I hope you're hungry. Joanna cooked us some ribs with garlic mashed potatoes and blueberry cobbler for dessert."

She clapped. "That's my daughter-in-love!"

We pulled into the drive way, and I could see the girls looking out the window, waiting for our arrival. Lily was jumping up and down, and I could see her mouth yelling, "Mom, they're here!"

Becca opened the door, just as Lily bolted out in front of her, running towards the car. "Daddy! Grandma! Yay! You're here!"

I gave Lily a huge hug and kiss, and then she raced around towards the passenger seat to my mother and did the same.

"Hey, Dad," Becca said, casually. I also gave her a hug and a kiss as I closed my door and unloaded the luggage. Becca helped my mother get out of the car and took her arm to walk her to the house, while Lily literally ran circles around them. Joanna was waiting by the door.

The ladies went in first, and I followed. Joanna and my mom greeted and kissed each other, while I awaited my love's kiss. She embraced me and kissed me quickly and softly.

The house smelled wonderful. I was going try to be optimistic and not think about the fact that two out of my five days went by without resting. I was going to do my best and enjoy the rest of the week with my family. Let Thanksgiving finally begin!

*****

On Sunday, we drove my mother to our nearby airport and realized that time sure went by too quickly. We all said our goodbyes and told my mother we loved her, were thankful she came to visit us, and that she was welcome anytime.

As Joanna drove us back home, I decided to cheat a little and text Sergeant Miller, asking him how he was doing, how many calls we got that week, and how many duty drives were done.

He responded almost immediately. "Sir, I'm glad you were able to enjoy the holidays with your family. We got 7 calls after work hours (Thursday-Sunday), and Chaplain Dubose had to drive to three of them. We were pretty busy. Don't think of that now. Enjoy the rest of your day with your family, and we'll see you tomorrow."

That meant it was going to be busy going back to work tomorrow, but at least I was able to enjoy Thanksgiving with my family—for that I was truly grateful. God had allowed things to happen the way they had for a reason. Thankfully, I was able to be there with my mom in her time of need, and she turned out to be just fine. We all gained 10 pounds. Last, but not least, I was able to enjoy some football.

Thanksgiving break had begun tragically—a suicide right before, then my mother's health scare. In the end, however, God knew how to care for me and bless me and, at the same time, His will was done.

Lord, forgive me for my selfishness, thinking only of and for myself and my family sometimes. Thank you for humbling me at all times and reminding me of Your grace and mercy. Thank you. Thank you. Thank you...

CHAPTER 11
~ Change of Plans ~

Jordan

The first week of January, the beginning of a new year, new memories, new outlook... The holidays were over, last year was gone, and I looked forward to new opportunities and progressing with everyone around me.

Joanna had been extremely sympathetic towards me and a bit harsh on the girls. I wasn't sure if it was the overconsumption of food the girls devoured, getting a little lazy, or the holiday candies and sweets having the opposite effect and hyping them into energizing bunnies. Regardless, I knew Lily and Becca were pleased to have enjoyed the holidays with me at home and the new gifts they received.

Speaking of which, dear Lord, girls are expensive, but thankfully easy to buy for. I was looking forward to filing taxes by the end of the month and refilling our pockets. The only next mild expenditure coming up would be Valentine's Day, which shouldn't be too hard to plan: hotel, dinner, a movie, etc. I couldn't help but think that maybe I should do something extra special with all Joanna had put up with and how much she had helped me in the last year. Yup, I needed to. She was always a step ahead of the game, and I should try harder, at least when I could.

Lily's birthday was right after Valentine's Day, so I'd coordinate with Joanna on what we should get her. Like I said before, easy but pricey.

Becca was done with volleyball season, so now she was focusing on her academics, along with studying for the SAT's. I was so proud of her! Becca was a smart, beautiful, young lady, and I prayed for my daughter's success, happiness, her future, her future husband... Lord, she was going to need a special kind of man: one that feared God and respected women. If Joanna was thought of as being strong and tough, Becca was twice as hard-hitting.

Speaking of strong women, another one had slowly been participating in congregational events more. Jennifer Nunes had been attending the chapel services after Thanksgiving, hoping to draw closer to and receive healing from God. She came up to me every Sunday, shook my hand, and had a radiant smile of gratitude. She had also eaten lunch with Joanna a few times. I was so glad she was seeking influence from a Godly woman.

Ms. Nunes had also been seeing Chaplain Simmons for emotional and spiritual counseling on a weekly basis. She originally had asked for me, but I just wasn't ready to playback that unfortunate event. It would haunt me too much. I knew myself well. I was happy she was moving forward with her life, but I was still struggling to sort through my own feelings.

She even asked me last Sunday when she should date again. I had explained to her that now was too soon. I did my best not to sound shocked, explaining that it was just my advice, that I was looking out for her, and that she was free to do as she pleased. However, getting into a relationship with a wounded heart, still so fresh, would be dangerous for both parties involved.

That following Monday, I made sure to mention it to Chaplain Simmons. I told him what she mentioned to me, simply as a courtesy, so that he would know how to handle it and guide her. She had a long road ahead of her, but so far, she was seeking wise counsel and making good progress. I was pleased for her.

*****

The first Tuesday of the New Year was upon us before I barely had a chance to blink. As I headed back to work, I drove with positive-inspirational music playing loudly, feeling quite up-beat and optimistic. I could feel joy in my heart, leftover bliss from the holidays.

As I walked into the chapel, I felt a sudden energy shift. There was a sense of foreboding, of something waiting for me, someone expecting something...? I didn't know quite what it was. I passed by

Sergeant Miller's office to quickly say hello, ask how he was doing, how Christmas was... the usual small talk.

Then, I opened my office door, placed my bag on the floor, and sat on my comfortable chair behind my desk. There was a sticky note placed on my computer screen that read: "Please come see me – Dubose." I sighed. Tuesday already felt like a Monday.

I walked slowly over towards his office, and I could see him on his computer. I knocked softly and gave a little wave as I entered his office. "Good Morning, sir! Happy New Year!"

He stood up walked around his desk, while saying, "Happy New Year, Jordan!" After a quick handshake, he said, "Please, sit down. I wanted to speak with you."

I sat on his couch, and he took a seat across from me in a large chair. I couldn't help but think that he was displaying mannerisms of a father about to talk to his to a son.

He started off by asking me how my holidays went, how my mother was doing, the girls, and so on—a good ten minutes of personal small talk. Still, I knew something was up; he was about to tell me something either huge or uncomfortable. He scooted his chair up and got cozy.

"Jordan, I wanted to talk to you first before you checked your email, since we both got the news at the same time. I just thought hearing it from me might be better than being bombarded with an apathetic message from the Pentagon.

He sighed and softened his voice. I furrowed my brows and braced myself for what he was going to say next. "You've been assigned to a 4-month deployment in Joint Base, Balad, Iraq, and you report February 5th."

He paused to see my reaction. He looked puzzled because I hadn't reacted at all. My mind still had not fully registered what he had just said. I knew my time was coming, but I had thought it would be in the summer. I now only had a few weeks to prepare.

He continued, "Also, we will be throwing you a farewell party on January 30th, as that will be your last day here. When you get back from Iraq, you'll have your reconstitution time off, obviously. The staff and I will be helping your family pack, because you've also been reassigned to Elmendorf AFB in Alaska, with a tentative report date of July 5th."

This time I naturally reacted with physical motion, putting my hands on my face with disbelief. I shook my head slightly, hoping the thoughts would jumble themselves back into place. When they didn't, I simply put my head down.

Chaplain Dubose immediately added, "I am so sorry, Jordan. I did the best I could for you. I even called headquarters to verify all the options. They had originally placed you to deploy in March for a 6-

month deployment, and then come back and move you to Germany. I thought this was the best alternative for you to be gone while your girls were in school, and then you can enjoy some of summer break with them."

I nodded, while I watched Dubose's hands fidget nervously. He cleared his throat. "Also, this was the best option for your advancement, as you will be the Deputy Wing Chaplain at Elmendorf now that you're a Major-Select."

Well, at least, there was a small bit of good news. All this information was a lot to digest. He tapped me on my knee and said, "If you need anything or have any questions, I am always here for you."

I mumbled a "thank you", and I walked numbly out of his office. Thoughts were flooding my mind. *Oh, man, I'm going to miss Valentine's Day with Joanna... Lily's birthday... Oh, no! Becca!*

I ran back towards Chaplain Dubose's office and blurted out, "Sir, my daughter has two years left of high school, could I apply for the High School Deferment so that she could graduate with her friends?"

"I don't think so, Jordan. She'd have to be a junior with a year left to qualify for that extension. I am sorry."

I replied with lamentation, "Ok, thank you, sir. And, I forgot to say so earlier: thank you for putting in a good word and doing the best that you could for me."

I returned to my office with mixed emotions. As I sat back at my desk, I turned on my computer to verify the breaking news. Skimming through my orders, there it was: Department of the Air Force... processed in DTS... TDY Length: 120 days... to Balad Air Base, Iraq. I closed the email and looked for my reassignment to Alaska. Alaska?! From Texas heat to Alaskan popsicles! Joanna hates cold weather. Lily likes adventures, so maybe she'd be ok with all of this. Rebecca—oh, my vocally opinionated teenage daughter, who was putting so much effort into her academics... she was going to be devastated.

Well, the 4 months I'm in Iraq, she would have time to process it all. Hopefully, she'd have time to get over it and accept it. Poor Joanna, she'd have to face Becca's wrath all by herself.

Iraq... Arg... This would be my third deployment and my first to the Middle East. The other two had been to South America and then East Africa. They were about the length of 5-6 months. Africa was the most memorable one since I was about 10 hours ahead. The ambiance and people were very indigenous, and I loved the wildlife surrounding the camp. However, I did come back sick from traveling plane to plane and having contact with so many people.

This was not how I wanted my new year to begin. I closed my door to pray and asked God for reassurance that this was His will. I also prayed for my girls at home that the Lord would soften and prepare their hearts for the tough year ahead.

After I finished praying, I looked at the calendar for the next possible weekend that I could plan a romantic getaway with Joanna to make up for Valentine's Day. "Ah ha!" I exclaimed out loud. "Yes!" Martin Luther King, Jr. Day would guarantee me a 3-day weekend. That didn't give me much time to plan, but I was going to do everything that I could to make it special for her... and to also plan something fun for the girls while we were away.

*****

The rest of the day flew by rather quickly. Before I knew it, I looked up and the clock read 5:03pm. I gathered my things and headed out towards my car. I called Joanna to tell her not to cook. I decided to take them out to dinner, asking Joanna and the girls to meet me at the restaurant of their choice.

I hoped that a fun restaurant would help soften the news of my deployment. Later, alone with Joanna, I would tell her about the move and discuss with her a good way to let the girls know.

I arrived at the restaurant they chose, and I could see the girls waiting for me at the entry way. Lily, of course, ran up to me and gave me a hug and a kiss as I picked her up and walked towards Joanna, giving both her and Rebecca a quick side hug and kiss.

As we got seated, I asked the girls how they were doing and how their day went. I also told them to order whatever they wanted— including Joanna, teasing her, asking if she wanted her Monday Merlot on Tuesday. I was not going to be frugal today, so I ordered an appetizer for the girls.

I felt slightly bad because they got cheery every time I encouraged them to get whatever they wanted. I was trying to be nice, but perhaps, it seemed that I was getting ready to tell them good news.

The waiter brought us our fried mozzarella sticks a few minutes later, and it was time to drop the bomb. "Honey, girls, you know that Daddy is active duty... and that means at any moment they could 'activate' me to deploy or leave for a while..." Joanna quickly squeezed my hand under the table with realization of what was about to be said next. "Remember when I had to leave for Africa for 5 ½ months? Well, it's that time again, where I have to leave..."

The girls were wide-eyed and quiet—the excitement of eating out quickly dissolved. Joanna sighed and asked with a tone of strained positivity, "Where? When?"

I took a bite of the mozzarella stick dipped in marinara sauce to buy myself some time and then softly answered, "Middle East... Iraq... only 4 months this time, though..."

Joanna quickly closed her eyes and turned her face away to avoid eye contact for a minute.

My ears began to ring, and I could feel my heart pounding in my throat as I blurted out the details: "This time I won't be in a camp. I'll be in a joint-base where I'm surrounded by army, air force, and all other branches, as well as allied countries participating in helping us combat terrorists. I will be landlocked. I leave on the 30th of this month from here and transport would probably stop in Spain, Germany, and two other stops, so I should arrive on the 2nd or 3rd. I report on the 5th."

I took a deep breath—all the bad news out in a rush. "Okay, girls, Joanna, I also talked to your mother today. Grandma Gracie will be arriving in 10 days to stay with you until the middle of February to help out."

At that news, Lily perked up. "Grandma Gracie? Yay!"

Joanna seemed unimpressed or maybe I was just misreading her facial expression as she picked at her appetizer, seeming to have lost her appetite.

"Baby, are you ok?" I asked quietly.

She looked up and our eyes met—a million words unspoken between us. "Yeah, honey, I felt this coming. I just didn't think it would be in January."

I took her hand in mine again. "Tentatively, I'll be back the first week of June. I'll get relieved as soon as another chaplain arrives, but I should be home sometime that first week for sure."

She managed to force a smile. "Okay, at least you'll be home for the summer, and we can plan a vacation."

I quickly stopped her there and whispered in her ear, "There's more to that when I come back. We've been reassigned. I'll talk to you about it when we get home, but don't mention summer please."

These are the times that I regret not calling her on the phone and just giving her a heads up. Her eyes got wide for just a moment. She blinked that she understood, and she put a smile on her face before turning back to the girls. "Well, this is all going to be an adventure for us, huh, girls? Don't worry. We are strong ladies. We will do our best to just get through the next few months until Daddy comes home. We got this, right?"

Becca shrugged at Joanna and I, but smiled down at Lily, who was waiting to see what her big sister's reaction to the news was going to be. "It'll be fine, Lily. We'll have some 'just for girls' fun. Maybe we could even have some of your friends over for a tea party...?"

Lily looked thrilled then. Becca, even with all her teenage angst, was a such a good big sister.

I gave Becca a smile of appreciation and bowed my head towards her in a motion of saying "thank you" without words. She had a strained smile on her face too, very similar to Joanna's, but she nodded back at me and winked her "you're welcome".

We all did our best to make small talk and enjoy the rest of our meal. I was proud of all my little ladies and their ability to adapt to change.

We finished up and got ready to leave the restaurant, after indulging in dessert too. I knew it was Tuesday and the girls had just returned to school from their winter break, but I decided to be spontaneous and rent a movie for them. Joanna was confused, but she didn't question me.

*****

We arrived home, and the girls scurried upstairs to shower and get ready for their movie.

As soon as Joanna and I were in our bedroom, we locked the door for privacy. Within a millisecond, Joanna blurted out a jumble of words, all in a rush, like they had been building up and needed to explode from her since she had heard the news. "Babe! Iraq?! I mean, in South America and Africa if you'd get captured, I know they'd make a trade or monetary deal, but in Iraq, those monsters will kill you. Their radical belief of Western culture, let alone

Christianity, will pin a target on your back. No, not your back, on your chest, since you wear that cross!"

I walked up to her and hugged her tightly. She began to release her anguish and cry. I comforted her with caressing and squeezing her tightly.

After a few moments, I whispered, "Shh, now, sweetheart. Pray that God will protect me and that I have a safe trip there and back. God is in control, and He knows what He is doing, even when we do not. I love you. Look at me. There now, everything will be fine."

She sniffled and wiped her nose on my shirt. I continued, "I'll be sure to try to call you when I'm allowed, or I'll email you every chance I get."

I took a deep breath. It was now or never. I had to tell her about Alaska too. "Also, I need you to sit. I have another announcement." I took her hand in mine, and we both sat, side by side, on the edge of the bed. "I also got PCS orders to Elmendorf when I return from Iraq."

She raised her eyebrows. "Elmendorf? Where's that?"

I gulped, "Alaska."

Her startled look would have been worth a million dollars. She inhaled and exhaled with a huge sigh. Then, she began to laugh at the ridiculousness of it all. "Well, instead of snakes and armadillos, I guess it'll be penguins and polar bears!"

I snickered, but I was relieved she was coming around. "I report to Elmendorf on July 5th, so we'll have a month to settle up north. Don't worry, Dubose told me he'd make sure to take care of you guys, help out with forms, and have everything shipped before I get back, so all we have to do is head up north and relax."

She nodded, taking all the information in. I gently rubbed her back and added, "I didn't think it was right to barrage the girls with two announcements, especially Becca."

With the bad news out of the way, I told her about the romantic weekend I had planned in order to cheer her up—which it did. She thanked me for the quick thinking on my part and for planning ahead all of the arrangements. In order to smooth out a convincing reasonable explanation for all the chaos, I told Joanna about my promotion to Deputy Wing Chaplain, as well. She was ecstatic for me. With her okay and by my side, everything was going to be alright.

*****

We picked up Grandma Gracie, Joanna's mother, at the airport—another strong woman added to my list of fierce queens. She was grateful for this trip, as she enjoyed helping and being around the girls.

We dropped her off at our house to get her acquainted and settled, and after an hour, Joanna and I left for our romantic destination. We were going to be staying in a remote area, far in the country, yet at a very luxurious resort. I wanted to spend time alone with my best friend and show appreciation in intimate ways.

Let the three-day holiday weekend begin!

*****

As we were headed back to our home from our much-needed mini vacation, the time was flying by quickly. I sorted in my head the checklist for deployment. I wasn't even home, and I could feel the anticipation.

Just like that, I knew to look over at the passenger side, and there I caught Joanna tear up a bit. The reality of what was to come must have hit us both instantaneously. Heartfelt tear drops from my sweetheart were difficult for me to bear, and my body wanted to comfort her and hold her. But for now, all I could do was grab her hand, pull it to my mouth, kiss it, and hold it tightly, while we continued the drive home.

CHAPTER 12
~ Leaving Home ~

Jordan

Grandma Gracie was still with us, but she decided to stay back at the house so that Joanna and the girls could drop me off at the DCC (Deployment Control Center) intimately. My arm was still sore from all the vaccinations last week, plus I had the headache of processing paperwork through different departments. It was all just very hectic.

We could see a gathering of families together, hugging, kissing, crying... I was always the one in the back comforting those who were saying farewell. My cheerleaders weren't cheering, but rather, they were quite gloomy at the notion of seeing me off.

I had talked to the girls separately, telling them how much I loved them, what I expected of them, etc. I also listened to what they hoped to accomplish in the next four months while I would be gone. I hugged them for a while, kissed them lots, and smiled one last time before I left them to head to my gate for a quick briefing, snacks, and to wait until it was time to board.

*****

After an hour of nonsense waiting, it was finally time to board the plane. I didn't expect the girls to want to stay, but knowing Joanna, they were probably parked by the gated fence to watch my plane take off. As I picked up my duffel bag, I scouted towards the tarmac, and there they were on the other side of the fence. Joanna was crying and blowing kisses. Becca stood there with a somber look, and Lily looked sad, but was waving with both hands.

As I boarded the plane and sat down, I finally broke. I bowed my head, as I tried to mask my tears. I wasn't crying because of where I was going or how long I'd be gone, but because I felt the uneasiness of my family. I rarely cried, but the heartfelt concept of separating from my family for a long time was so difficult to fathom.

A man could work satisfactorily knowing his domain was being taken care of alright. Having peace of mind going into deployment was the best calming compound soldiers could have for going into work and performing their best.

I normally explained this to a lot of spouses at my sermons, marital counseling, or benedictions: Don't overwhelm the Airmen with unnecessary problems, drama, or issues that could be resolved domestically rather than overseas.

When I was deployed the last two times, most of the crew hung around together and watched TV to feel united and lifted, and I had quite a few come see me for advice because their wives were "nagging" them for attention, which was quite common. Time apart was mostly hard on the spouses (especially with kids), because they had to do everything on their own—interact alone, handle all domestic issues by themselves, take over the other spouses' regular chores. It was additional work.

Although the Airmen most likely missed their families, they had someone to talk to, eat with, work with, etc., while deployed. They were never quite alone or had privacy, but they did have support.

When two parties were in different atmospheres for a while from their respective homogeneous daily rituals, it could agitate one or both since the "union" had been parted for a while. In mature relationships, it helped the couple realize not to take each other for granted, to learn appreciation for one another, and to work on communication skills, since they would have a lack of physical touch for months, sometimes years, at a time. Those were the guys that did well in deployments—those with supportive spouses. They were the happiest, the most productive, stress-free, and usually got the most recognition.

I knew that the girls would be active with school, but as for Joanna, I had asked her to do me a few favors while I was gone to keep her busy and not dwell in my absence.

On Tuesdays, I had asked her to do a ladies' Bible study in the morning and, then, afterwards to go out to lunch with them. On Wednesdays, there was the mid-week worship and family night at the chapel, and I asked her to make sure to attend with the girls and enjoy a free night of not having to cook since the chapel provided dinner.

On Thursdays (anytime of the day), I asked her to visit Ms. Stanley, an elderly widow who came into my office every two weeks and brought me homemade muffins. In return, I would often spend an hour or so keeping her company in her home to reciprocate in appreciation and to cheer up a little, old lady who didn't have family nearby.

When March rolled around, I requested that Joanna make the most of "Spring Cleaning" and throw out junk and stuff that wasn't necessary and start packing our belongings secretly, unless we had agreed to tell the girls before then. We still weren't sure when the best time to do that was going to be.

As I was one of the first to board the plane, I could see a few Airmen that were seated with their bags in their lap—fresh younglings out of high school, just 18-year-olds.

I really disagreed with the age entry of 18 into the armed forces; it should be 20 or 21. At 18, their brains were not fully developed, and their hormones were still actively adjusting, while maturing.

However, if age couldn't be changed, then at least wait and give them 2-3 years of training domestically. Then, they could be sent out on TDY's. When they reached their age of "war entry", then they could deploy.

It would minimize and lower the cost of training and re-training, and it would reduce human-error by a huge percentage. It would also decrease medical costs. There is a huge difference in sending an 18-year-old to war vs. a 22-year-old. Although PTSD could affect anyone, a teenager, whose brain and body were still adjusting, would have a greater chance of having PTSD than, say, a 22-year-old.

I decided to get myself out of my funk and to introduce myself to the younglings while we waited for the rest to board. Some were scared. Some were trying to look brave. Some looked excited. Regardless, it surprised me to think that just last year, in high school, their mommas made them sandwiches for lunch. Now, this year, they were ready for combat.

Glancing around, my eye caught a young girl, at the most 20 years old. She reminded me so much of my Rebecca. I could not imagine what her father must be feeling—his baby girl, going to war, surrounded by men. I began to pray for her and for my Rebecca. I hoped she could someday forgive me for all the moving, adjusting into different school systems, restarting her life, and so much more...

*****

After 2 hours of waiting, I had to stand up and run to the bathroom. I should have gone before I boarded. However, when I realized the C17 was about to take off, I knew I couldn't wait. I made my apologies for the delay and did my best to hurry. They let me. No one likes to say no to the chaplain. I grinned.

As I sat back down, the pilots told us to rest, since we would be stopping in Norfolk, VA to pick up more soldiers and stall for a couple of hours, then our next stop would be in Frankfurt, Germany. After that, we would be landing briefly at Al Udeid Air Base, Qatar, and then off to my final destination: Balad Air Base.

This was going to be a looooooong trip, with many delays and long days. I began to pray silently for safety, guidance, wisdom, and God's grace over me. I also prayed for my girls. And, that's where my passion elongated the prayer in my mind...

CHAPTER 13
~ Trust and Obey ~

<u>Rebecca</u>

The drive home from the airport was a quiet and somber one. My mom had turned on some worship music, and she was softly singing and crying. I looked back at Lily in the backseat. Her eyes were blinking slower and slower, and I knew that soon she would be asleep. I envied her.

My heart was heavy. Dad worked a lot, and we didn't always see him often during the week, but I always knew that he would be there if we needed him. It was hard to imagine 4 months without him.

Mom was going to be busy doing her "wifey" duties, so I knew already that a lot of the responsibility to look after Lily was going to fall on me. Thankfully, volleyball season was over, but I had a lot of schoolwork and studying to focus on. I could feel the stress and emotions begin to overwhelm my brain and body, and I remembered to take a deep breath.

"You okay?" Mom asked.

"Yah, I guess…" I shrugged.

She reached over the center console and patted my knee. "I know it's hard, but everything will be just fine. God is in control. His plan for our lives hasn't changed one bit, just our perception of it. We are exactly where we are meant to be."

Like an arrow to my heart, her words, for some reason, pierced through my tough armor. That really made a lot of sense to me. If I would knock it off with having a bad attitude and worrying about things all the time, I could find peace in knowing I was exactly where God wanted me to be.

I closed my eyes and prayed to God to help me to be strong for Lily, to not get easily frustrated with her, to be able to retain the information from my schoolwork, and to soften my heart and help me to be the woman I'm meant to be.

Ha! Even I thought that was a pretty mature prayer. I really did want all those things, but it was hard to keep my emotions in check sometimes. Like Mom had said, maybe I just needed to change my perception of things and better adapt. The Big Man upstairs knew what He was doing.

The old Sunday School song "Trust and Obey" popped into my head: "Trust and obey, for there's no other way, to be happy in Jesus, but to trust and obey..."

Well, if it was good enough for kindergarteners, it should be applicable for me as well. Sometimes, easier said than done. But, I was really going to work hard at simply trusting in God and obeying.

I closed my eyes once more and added a little bit extra to my earlier prayer. Because of my innate selfishness and being a self-absorbed teenager, I had completely forgotten to ask God to watch over my dad.

Please, God, keep him safe. Help him so that he can help others. Protect him and bring him home to us. In Your name, I pray. Amen.

CHAPTER 14
~ The Battle Within ~

Jordan

Finally, after four, tiresome, shower-less days, we arrived at Balad Air Base. I walked into processing with my orders and got acquainted in my dorm room. I tried to find access to a computer for me to email Joanna, to let her know that I made it safe and sound, that I would be taking a long sleep, and that I would contact her again when I could.

I ate quickly. I showered. I was very drowsy and fatigued. I crashed into bed and proceeded to sleep for the next 10 hours.

*****

After a long sleep, I woke up with consternation—a sudden realization that I was in Iraq. I sat up to ask God for time to go by quickly, for me to be a blessing onto others here, and for my family to be well cared for while I was away.

I got acquainted with my schedule, and then I met and greeted all the commanders. Sitting with them, I elaborated on the importance of spiritual morale—encouraging the soldiers to attend a service to get a positive message and for motivation, cleansing, and a united coalition.

When I left their building, I went over to speak to security forces; they had a special place in my heart for all that they did. They risked their lives for our safety and guarded us at all costs. They were the front-men as well our protection.

As I met each and every one of them, I felt God slowing me down, to heed and wait for the next shift to begin and to greet those coming in. So, I waited one more hour until the Spirit led me.

As the next shift began, all guards sat down for their briefing. As they were talking about what the next plans would be for the next few days, the Senior Master Sergeant said that we had a new operation coming up and that things would be changing constantly. He then introduced Staff Sergeant Crimson to explain the new implementations of this precarious task.

My breath was drawn, and I felt the Spirit of God pressing me down against the chair. I could almost audibly here God say to me: "Him."

After the meeting was adjourned, I walked up to Sergeant Crimson and introduced myself to him. He seemed like a nice young man. There was something about him that reminded me of someone. His eyes, his nose, his facial features were familiar. I made a mental note to run into Sergeant Crimson as much as I could.

*****

After a few days had passed, I was requested by the 54th Squadron Commander and Assistant Director of Operations for an urgent meeting. I sat down with Lieutenant Colonel Ferry and Major Brown to discuss a matter regarding one of their pilot's behavior.

Captain Higgins had endured a trauma that had stalled him from performing his duties, and he refused to see the mental health specialist/psychologist, because although it's confidential, it would go on record. With a chaplain, however, there would be no paper trail.

Captain Higgins was struggling to deal with this emotional block and was scared that it would impact his career if the psychologist discharged him to leave early from deployment. They briefly told me what they thought it could be, but there was no assurance or breakthrough that had happened.

I agreed to approach Captain Higgins and see if he would talk to me, additionally notifying him that he was more than welcome to speak with me in 100% confidentiality, with no reprimand. I also told them I'd join their squadron for lunch and dinner to make my presence better known and socialize as a peer and support structure.

After 3 days, Captain Higgins finally approached me and asked if he could meet with me the next day to speak about a delicate subject. I, of course, agreed.

To be honest, I hadn't been keeping up with the calendar days. We kept up with time, which was crucial. The base was 24-hour operational on last minute changes. As 0900 came near, I finished writing Joanna an email to let her know that I was doing well, that the first month of being deployed was almost near, and that meant we only had 3 months left.

Captain Higgins knocked on my door a bit early, but I was expecting him. I closed my laptop and greeted him warmly. "Come in, Captain Higgins."

He sat down apprehensively and began, "Sir, I was suggested to speak with you regarding this ordeal that won't allow me to fly and perform my mission. I'm not sure how to forget this torment that was incredibly terrible for me to listen to a couple of weeks ago…"

I asked him first to talk a bit about his childhood, his background, and his faith status. He told me that he came from a divorced family, decent middle class, and rarely went to church, just on Easter and Christmas. The typical American that "believed there's a God" but hadn't attempted to get close to Him.

I reiterated to him that what we would speak of did not go beyond the four walls and that everything was completely confidential. That seemed to put him at ease. So, he sat back, took a deep breath, and I listened to his story...

"As you know, sir, I fly classified missions. This last one has not left me at peace, won't let me sleep, or even move on. 3 weeks ago, we were Supporting a mission over Fallujah. We were tasked with following a courier back to a possible terrorist training facility."

I nodded for him to continue.

"We followed him to a Madrasa, where we identified three armed Al-Qaeda members in a walled off courtyard on the back of the building. Our tasking was to take out the three terrorists, but as you would know, being so close to a school makes that impossible to bomb without knowing how many children could be inside. About an hour passed and one of the men came out with a child, a boy. Fortunately for our intel, but unfortunately for me, the man's radio must have been stuck on, because I could hear everything the man and boy were saying.

Captain Higgins inhaled deeply as he began cry a bit. "Well, as you know, we have contract interpreters that listen to enemy radio communications to help decipher, and the boy was yelling, 'Please! Please! No! It hurts!' I just..."

He began to weep for a few moments and then resumed. "We heard the child's cry, screaming, begging for the men to stop..."

Captain Higgins cleared his throat and wiped the tears from his eyes. "I was ready to obliterate those men." A touch of anger filled his tone. "But, we couldn't. Ironically, because of the presence of the child had just confirmed the potential collateral damage in that building. To make matters worse, our rules of engagement do not legally allow us to defend an Iraqi civilian. Raping children is considered an 'accepted practice' in their culture..."

I, too, became saddened by what Captain Higgins was saying. "It is unfortunate what we have to see or hear when we're at war, and I'm sorry you had to experience that."

I waited for a few moments before asking the next delicate question. "Let me ask you: Were you molested as a young child?"

Still lightly whimpering, he shook his head and inserted, "No... but my dad was... and he became an abusive alcoholic. I can't help but think, because we didn't end that child's misery, what kind of monster will he become? The agony and bitterness will subvert his soul... Sir, reading about these stories, hearing about them from comrades... I would have been able to handle it. But it played out live, while I was able to do something! I could have stopped it!"

Captain Higgins sighed, seemingly exhausted by speaking of the horror out loud. "I don't know. It makes me rethink my career. Have you had to deal with a situation that was life or death or try to prevent a tragedy... but you just couldn't?"

At that moment, I felt God scolding me for questioning Him about last year's incident with the Nunes family. He knew I could answer that question. He knew that the experience I dealt with could help others.

I told Captain Higgins what happened to me last year and that for me I found solace in God. I knew that I had my wife and family for support, but since we were in combat, with no comfort of being at home, or family, asking God for help was our human right and could be done at anytime, anywhere.

I asked Captain Higgins if he didn't mind if I began a prayer, and he said he did not. I placed one hand on his shoulder, and we both bowed our head and closed our eyes...

"Dear Lord, Heavenly Father, we come before you to first and foremost ask for forgiveness for our transgressions, for we are merely humans. We are innately selfish beings, with improper thoughts and actions, so please cleanse us of our emotions, mind, and soul so that we can be purified and live for You gracefully.

"Lord, I bring forth Captain Higgins. God, you know his pain and heartache. You know what he's had to endure over and over. We humbly ask that You please help him and heal him, to be able to have courage and strength to continue his missions, for we now see the evil we face—dirty and wicked. Help him understand it was not his fault, God, that he was doing his job and justice shall be done for that little boy.

"Protect that young boy. Heal and guide him. Reveal yourself to him so that he knows Your power and mercy to transform into a new creature.

"Lord, unload that baggage from Captain Higgins. Clear his mind, give him peace, and fill him with Your love so that he can see Your truth. We pray this prayer in faith, in the name of Jesus. Amen."

I opened my eyes, and although he didn't make sound or motion, I could see tears rolling down his face. I waited for his response.

Finally, he said softly, "Thank you, sir. I hope He hears your prayer, because I know I haven't been a 'holy' person."

I smiled. "The first step in getting better is admitting you have an issue to deal with. You're here, seeking help. That's excellent. God has heard your plea. Think about Him. Talk to Him. Seek Him, and watch how He will work in your life for you. He will help you to find joy again."

Captains Higgins seemed to relax as I spoke, so I continued. "Listen, you can come to me at any time. Please feel free to find me. That's why I'm here. I'll be praying for you tonight. Let's find things we can occupy ourselves with, too, so we don't dwell on the past with the free time we have on our hands sometimes.

"If you need a book to read, I have plenty, but I challenge you to start with the Bible. It contains soothing, consoling words that God speaks to us through. Start with John 16:33 tonight. It says this:

> *These things I have spoken to you, that in Me you may have peace. In the world you will have tribulation; but be of good cheer, I have overcome the world.*

"Let him guide you. Praying can be the internal voice that directs the external action. Also, don't forget our chapel services that we have are listed on your MWR (morale, welfare, and recreation) board. Please, come and attend. I'll be talking this Sunday..."

He nodded and shook my hand with a confident grip. He thanked me once more and left my office.

As he closed the door, I did breakdown a little on the inside, as I couldn't imagine his situation. Children were the key to Heaven's lock. Anyone that inflicted harm on them should be (in my opinion) destined to go straight to hell.

I cleared my mind and began to thank God for allowing me to help that young man, to ask God for forgiveness if I did offend Him for placing blame on Him for last year's circumstances. I thanked Him for everything. I acknowledged that His will was perfect and that He knew the plan before we were born. I also prayed for Him to give me strength for whatever was to come...

*****

After two days, Lieutenant Colonel Ferry came to my office to get feedback on Captain Higgins and whether or not, in my opinion, he had a true detrimental trauma (PTSD) to the point where he should be sent back home.

I asked him in return, "Well, has he been more forthcoming or social?"

He nodded. "Yes, better, helping out and keeping busy..."

I explained, "Captain Higgins did go through some emotional shock, but I am not a licensed medical professional to diagnose him with PTSD. In my opinion, if he is improving, give him a couple more days and observe him. If he's regressing, then it's your call."

He shook my hand and said, "Thank you, Chaplain. Let's hope he goes to your service tomorrow."

I injected, "You know, sir, if you want to be there for Captain Higgins and support him, if you could, perhaps you could also attend the service with him to show him you care for his well-being..."

He smiled. "I intend to do just that, sir."

*****

The next day, Sunday, I got up early to ask God for words of encouragement for the Airmen and that He would speak through me, open their hearts, and elevate their spirit. I prayed that worship would be profuse and rich for Him, just like it was with King David in times of war, and that He would send His spirit to be with us.

Since base was 24-hour operational, I would be speaking every 3 hours for the first 12 hours, and the other chaplain who had the night shift would do the same.

The first service was at 0800 in the morning. There were not a lot of attendees, but it went well. I did not see Captain Higgins or Lieutenant Colonel Ferry. The second service rolled around at 1100, and boy, was that one packed! It was a great service, and I felt God's presence. I was overwhelmed by God's grace and atonement. I hoped the next one would be just as powerful. However, truth be told, I was getting tired and hungry.

I ducked out for a few minutes to eat lunch with the guys, and I decided to take a quick power nap. I woke up refreshed, and optimistic for the next service and that I would see Captain Higgins and Lieutenant Colonel Ferry.

As we were about to begin, I scanned the rows of seats. There they were! And, not just the two of them, but Major Brown had joined them as well. I caught Captain Higgins' eye and gave him a little wave. And, with that, I began my service by reading God's Word, John 16:33.

*****

After a couple of weeks had gone by, Lieutenant Colonel Ferry came into my office and wanted to personally thank me for encouraging him to attend that service with his adjutants.

He told me, "I wasn't going to attend as I was extremely busy and tired from working that day, but something in me pushed me to do so. And my decision had led Major Brown to follow—out of courtesy or impression, I don't know. Regardless, it was a positive domino-effect. I was close to sending Captain Higgins home since it's easier to replace a 'defective' soldier than to wait around for him to improve. However, this decision led to a much better outcome.

"Not only has Captain Higgins turned completely around, he has also been dedicated to developing new tactics, techniques, and procedures for his fellow pilots. Additionally, he has become quite encouraging and an overall morale booster to his fellow comrades. I had little faith, but it happened anyways."

I smiled and responded, "Sir, all it takes is just a little faith. When our leaders become selfless to our Airmen, you don't enhance one, but you enhance them all. To lead is to serve our own. A shepherd always takes care of his sheep in order for the pack to continue the walk. Morale goes up. Your men will trust they can count on you. Knowing that they can come to you gives them confidence that you just won't 'dispose' of them. The battle begins with oneself..."

CHAPTER 15
~ Visual Aids ~

<u>Joanna</u>

After spending Valentine's Day with the girls and my mom, I yearned for Jordan, and I hoped that he was doing well in Iraq. Although it was a nice gesture of Jordan to have my mom stay and help with the girls for a month, it was even more difficult with the sudden realization that now my mother had left too. I felt very alone and on my own.

Little did I know, though, Jordan had contacted my friends, so they'd call me more often to visit and keep me busy. One of my closest friends, Aleisha—a sassy, out-spoken chichi of a woman who could make it shine in the rainiest of days—took it upon herself to take me out for my birthday.

Aleisha arrived early enough to help me get dressed, knowing that I probably wouldn't be in the mood to go out and that I was too tired to really make any decisions for myself.

Of course, Aleisha, being the sensational friend that she is, spurred me on, "Nuh-uh, honey, we are going out for your birthday. You staying here will very much let 'loneliness' win this battle. The girls will be fine, Becca is 15 and can watch Lily for two hours. It ain't going to kill her."

It was the push I needed. She helped me with my wardrobe, hair, and make-up. It did lift my spirits a little, and ultimately, I did feel good about myself.

We decided to go to my favorite seafood restaurant. It was actually quite nice to wind down, catch up, and talk with someone about life and the prospect of moving to Alaska. I feared the unknown—new living style, new atmosphere, starting over, the cold weather, etc. However, I reassured Aleisha that all I really needed to be happy was God, Jordan, and my girls.

I shared my concerns about Lily, but I spoke mostly of Becca, moving to a whole new time zone, leaving her friends, and worrying about continuing to focus even while being interrupted. School transferring was always a hassle, but it could be done, hopefully without too much extra effort.

We were having so much fun that we had forgotten about the time. Aleisha asked the waiter for the check.

I said, "Please don't. You don't have to take care of this. You've done so much already."

Aleisha laughed. "Girl, I'm not! Your hubby sent me the gift card already, so it's on him!"

I just couldn't believe it. Jordan had thought of everything. He was such a good husband.

The waiter passed by and handed them the check. Aleisha was quick, and as usual, rather loud to ask, "Hey, sweetheart, do you guys give military discount? Her husband is deployed, and it's her birthday tonight. It would really make our day a little brighter..."

The waiter shrugged his shoulders and said, "I don't think so, but let me ask my manager."

He came back about a minute after, and says, "I'm sorry it's only for active-duty members and they have to be in uniform, but he did offer a free birthday dessert...?"

Aleisha raised her eyebrows, took a deep breath, and I knew she was about to go off and say more in dispute. Before she could begin what I knew would be one of her famous tirades about injustices, I gave her a little kick under the table, and graciously accepted his offer. She "hrumpphhed", crossed her arms, and pouted for a minute like a sullen toddler. She got over it rather quickly, though, when the dessert menu came.

I picked out my favorite dessert. We devoured it and didn't feel sorry even a little bit. Calories don't count on your birthday. It was delicious.

As we finished, the waiter came back and gave the gift card back to Aleisha. "Ma'am, a couple of people overheard you asking about the military discount. They mentioned that they were praying for your family. Someone else has paid your bill tonight."

His smile got bigger. "In addition, a few customers pitched in and purchased these for you as well." He set 3 additional gift cards in front of me. "They wanted to make sure that I told you, 'Thank you for your service'."

My eyes began to water in gratitude and surprise. Every once in a while, humanity really could surprise me. I was so very grateful.

Aleisha sure made my birthday memorable, intentionally and unintentionally. She was given a mission by Jordan, and she succeeded in completing it to the fullest.

*****

As I attempted to follow this new schedule that Jordan had requested of me, I took the girls to the Wednesday night chapel service for the first time since Jordan had left. At first, I was a bit apprehensive, since I usually avoided driving at night. But, I did it for Jordan. It made me feel closer to him somehow.

We ate the community dinner, socialized, worshiped, and listened to the brief message. I was in awe of how well it went.

As the girls and I were getting ready to drive out of the parking lot, I saw Bryan Doherty from the worship team walking out of the chapel and decided to have a quick word with him.

"Aren't you cold? Where are you heading to?"

His teeth chattered a bit. "Yes, ma'am, it's cold. I'm just heading to my dorm. It's only about 2 miles from here."

"Oh, that's silly. It's far too cold tonight. Hop on in. We'll give you a ride."

He hurried over to their vehicle and opened the back-left seat. "Hi, Lily!" he said to her in the back seat. Then, he added, "Hey, Becca!" and gave her a playful thump on the shoulder.

He put his seatbelt on quickly, and gushed, "Oh, thank you, Mrs. Ramonda. You really didn't have to do this. I'm okay walking, but I appreciate it very much."

I shook my head. "No, honey, it's no problem. Plus, I don't want you out getting sick. Do you have any form of transportation, like a bike?"

He replied with a cheerful tone, despite his answer. "Nah, I'm a bit broke right now, so I'm saving up again."

I immediately remembered what he meant by 'again'. His ex-fiancé had used him to buy her all the things she wanted and eventually dumped him—hence, his wariness about dating again.

As we approached his dorm, which was literally a 2-minute drive, he got out and said, "Thank you, Mrs. Ramonda and girls. You and your husband are one of a kind."

I asked, "Ha! What do you mean? I hope that's a good thing..."

Just before he got out of the car, he piped, "Well, you know, Chaplain J always gives me a ride after chapel services..."

I smiled and waved. I learned of yet another one of many charitable deeds my husband did for others. So, every Wednesday, I decided to go a step further and pick up Bryan from his dorm, too, and drop him off after the service. The girls began to grow fond of him—his personality, sense of humor... They grew to like him as an older brother.

CHAPTER 16
~ For Such a Time... ~

<u>Joanna</u>

One Thursday morning, Lily woke up with a fever. She probably had caught the virus from Wednesday night, since that was where the usual exchanging of hugs and handshakes occurred the most.

I had been tracking her fever since 7am, and I made sure to check on her hourly until 3pm when it was consistently warm. Lily began to shiver and shake; her symptoms and temperature worsened. So, I decided to take Lily to the base clinic for urgent care.

As we arrived, we saw the waiting line was long, but we still checked-in. As 4:30pm neared, the nurse called me up to the front desk and said they were sorry, but most likely they wouldn't be able to see Lily.

Upset, I asked through clenched teeth, "What do you mean you can't see my daughter? Because it's almost time to leave? Why didn't you tell me that at check-in, so I could have gone to a civilian clinic?"

I was so upset. I picked up Lily, and as we walked out of the clinic, I burst into tears. Not being able to do anything for poor, sweet, sick Lily and not having Jordan's assistance for times like this made me feel so helpless.

As I kept on walking, trudging our way back to the car, I suddenly turned the corner bumped into someone - Captain Bailey.

"Mrs. Ramonda? Hey, what's wrong?!"

I did my best to wipe off my teary face while still holding Lily. I explained the situation to her and how devastated and overwhelmed I was feeling.

Captain Bailey immediately gave us a quick hug and told us to follow her and that she would guarantee that Lily would be seen upstairs by one of her doctors.

I was a bit perplexed at what kind of authority she had, so I said, "Captain Bailey, I don't want to be a bother, really. I'm sorry. I really didn't mean to get you involved in this whole mess. I just needed someone to vent to..."

Captain Bailey didn't turn around and kept walking with a stern confidence as we followed meekly behind her. "Nonsense, Mrs. Ramonda, don't worry about a thing. I'm the Clinic Health Administrator."

I was a bit shocked I hadn't learned this information before, but I was very grateful this miracle came through, I almost felt hopeless and defeated.

Captain Bailey took us through the back-way and down a hallway, like some sort of VIP treatment. She asked one of the doctors to please come see Lily. We only waited about 10 minutes, and Lily was seen and treated. They prescribed her some antibiotics, and Captain Bailey personally took us downstairs to make sure that even the pharmacy would take care of us, since it was so close to their 5pm closing time.

After I received Lily's medication, my mind was still reeling. I just couldn't believe how well everything had worked out. Words could not express the gratitude I felt towards Captain Bailey. I thanked her, sincerely, with a huge hug.

Captain Bailey, without hesitation, said, "Mrs. Ramonda, you're certainly welcome. If you need anything else at all, please give me a ring, and I'll personally take care of it. This is the least I could do for you guys. Chaplain Ramonda has helped me and my husband work on our marriage, and I'm ever grateful."

Her phone rang, and she signaled me to wait just a moment. I took a few steps away to give her privacy, but I could still overhear her husband on the phone. "Hey, babe, everything ok?"

Captain Bailey responded, "Yes, honey, I'm done now. I'll be outside in 2 minutes. I just need to run upstairs and grab my bag."

After she hung up, she turned to Lily and me and again reiterated that she hoped Lily felt better soon and if we needed anything, we should call her. She asked us to also please excuse her, that she wanted to stay and chat, but that her husband was waiting outside to take her out for dinner. We warmly hugged one last time and then went our separate ways.

As I walked out and got a very sleepy Lily settled in the vehicle, in my peripheral view, I saw Captain Bailey come out of the building and approach her husband's car. I couldn't help but smile as I watched them greet each other and kiss with a light-heartedness and whimsy that was not seen in their relationship previously.

I was glad Captain Bailey's marriage was improving, and I made a mental promise to not complain in the future when Jordan invited people over to our home for a meal. It reminded me of one of Jordan's favorite quotes: "Selfless acts are blessings in disguise..."

CHAPTER 17
~ Spring Break ~

<u>Rebecca</u>

I had been feeling rather complacent and laid back lately. I wasn't sure if it was the peace that I had prayed for or a lack of passion. I needed something to get me out of my funk.

I had been left alone, for the most part, to deal with my responsibilities and to make sure Lily was okay, while Dad was deployed. I had also been focusing on my SAT prep courses and driving practice with Mom.

With spring break nearing, I hoped that Mom would let us do something fun. Maybe have some friends over for a little party or something. I wasn't sure exactly what I wanted to do, but I really needed something to look forward to.

As the time neared, I knew that the way to approach Mom about it was to help her to realize that I wanted to make the most of our time together. I knew the way to spin it was by asking her for a "girl's time" event that would make some happy memories.

Over dinner that night, Mom asked Lily and I what we wanted to do for spring break. Lily, of course, went with her usual every-year-answer of Disney World, while I requested that we all go to the beach with some friends.

After a bit of planning and moving funds around, Mom surprised us. She had found a way to combine the best of both worlds and booked a Disney cruise for us to enjoy. We were ecstatic. Mom was even able to make arrangements for Lily and me to also invite one friend to tag along.

When the time came, we all had an amazing time. However, there was a diminutive bleak moment every day when it was "Family Dinner Time", thinking about how much we missed Dad. But, then, one of us would do or say something silly, and the moment faded while we all ate.

At dinner one night, Mom also sat us down and explained that we would be moving to Alaska when Dad got back. He had been reassigned there. My initial response was to automatically be upset, but then I realized that maybe a move would be a good thing. A fresh start might be a positive change. I had been growing bored, feeling ambiguous about life and the future.

This cruise had been the most exciting thing to happen in a long time, and I definitely felt closer to Mom and even Lily. Maybe God did know what He was doing and knew we needed an adventure in another state. I determined in my heart to try and stay positive and not gripe and complain.

There wasn't much else to do in Alaska other than study. Ha! So, maybe it would help me better prepare for my SATs. My big focus right now was in getting into a good college.

I was so thankful to Mom for making the cruise happen. I felt a bit spoiled, but we all had so much fun. It was a much-needed vacation for all of us. It made the time with Dad away seem to go by more quickly. We only had about 2 ½ months left until he was going to come home!

CHAPTER 18

~ Open Doors ~

Joanna

After the cruise, on a Tuesday night, at ladies' Bible study, the ladies at the chapel planned an all ladies Saturday brunch get-together. One of the newest attendees, Jennifer Nunes announced she wished to come, but didn't have a babysitter for her 3-year-old, Henry. One of the ladies suggested that she just bring him to brunch, but Jennifer explained that he got grumpy around that time, since that was right around his nap time.

I approached Jennifer and told her to bring Henry over to our house, volunteering Becca to watch him. Plus, Lily loved to play big sister to toddlers. She happily agreed, and arrangements were all set.

*****

As Saturday morning approached, Jennifer and Henry arrived at our home a bit earlier than expected, so as they came in, I set up the TV for Henry and Lily. Once they were settled, I gave Jennifer a quick tour around the house to assure her that it would be safe.

Becca was ready for the responsibility, although she was initially annoyed when I notified her that she was volun-told to babysit on a Saturday morning, but she perked up and seemed excited to do it when she was promised a compensation afterwards.

Becca came out into the living room, just as Jennifer and I were getting our coats on to leave. She smiled warmly. "Hello, Ms. Nunes, don't worry. We're going to have a happy morning together, aren't we?"

Both Lily and Henry nodded, as Becca continued, "Have fun, and don't worry about anything. I'll call if I have any questions or need anything."

"Thanks so much, Becca," Jennifer replied, with a smile of relief on her face.

*****

As Jennifer and I rode together to the brunch meeting, the conversation turned to the power of prayer, healing, and moving on from the tragedy that Jennifer had faced with her husband's suicide.

Jennifer explained, "I've been attending counseling. I truly believe that God has healed my heart from that awful day. May I ask you something?"

"Of course, anything..." I replied as I turned into the restaurant parking lot.

She hesitated for a moment and then asked, "When do you think it would be appropriate for me to begin dating again?"

I wasn't exactly sure how to answer her, so I answered her question with another question. "Jennifer, are you sure that's something that you want to get into so soon? Are you in a hurry to marry again?"

"Well..." Jennifer seemed to contemplate the questions asked of her. "...I'm not in a hurry. But I really do want a life partner. Robert and I never really had that in our marriage. We were so disconnected that it really never felt like we were a real couple, you know?"

I could understand that. I replied gently, "Yes, that makes sense. Honestly, I can't answer the question of 'when' for you. That's between you and God. But what I do know is that there is no rushing God's perfect timing. Be patient. He has a plan. Perhaps continue to figure out yourself and spend some more time healing, and have faith that He will bring you a new life partner..."

Jennifer nodded. "I know you're right, Joanna. It's just, it's not about me, really. It's about Henry. I want him to have a father figure. My father was not a great father, and in learning all this with counseling, it's what led me to fall for a 'broken' man. I don't want Henry growing up without a father, let alone a broken mother."

As I parked the car, I replied, "Jennifer both my husband and I were raised by single mothers. You bet it was hard, but it can be done. You're not broken, and your will is strong. You love Henry, and you are strong enough to fight for him. You're still learning to realize your mistakes and better yourself in every aspect you can. You've been doing the right thing and taking courageous steps, seeking counseling, meeting with other women, attending services, seeing how the spiritual leaders live their lives righteously, etc. Show Henry the best woman you can be. Focus on that. When he grows up, he'll want a woman like his mother, and what kind of woman do you want her to be?"

She looked at me in what seemed to be disbelief, and I worried that I had gone too far.

"Well, I had never thought of it like that. Thank you, Joanna." she gushed. "That is really what I needed to hear. Thank you."

I felt the eagerness and willingness of Jennifer to better herself, and I said a quick prayer with her there in the parking lot that God would bless her relationship and her future husband as well, when and/or if that was His will.

The ladies' brunch meeting was a wonderful time. I mentioned to Jennifer that on Wednesdays they had a family night at the chapel and provided a free dinner. Jennifer had heard that, but she hadn't yet attended. She happily thanked me for reminding her, took the offer, and said she'd meet the girls and me on Wednesday.

*****

As Wednesday evening began, Jennifer searched the crowd and sat down next to me. She whispered in my ear that she wanted to sit by me because I would know all the right people to meet and get acquainted with. I was touched that she thought so much of me.

I did my best to introduce everyone at the dining gathering to Jennifer. Even Chaplain Simmons was there and was surprised to see her.

He tapped me on the shoulder and whispered, "I didn't even think about asking Ms. Nunes to come on Wednesdays, thanks. That may even help better with our sessions, so we can schedule on Wednesdays too!" He patted me on the back, and I knew what he meant. Sometimes counseling sessions could take longer, and even though he knew that they must end by 5pm, it would give him a few minutes of overlap if needed.

As we finished up, Bryan came to find us so that we could make our ritual brief car ride to his dorm. Jennifer was walking with me and the girls, and I introduced her casually to Bryan, not thinking anything of it.

They shook hands and said polite "hellos", and we all parted ways. As Jennifer led an excited Henry to their car, I could hear him chatting excitedly about everything that he had learned in the child's class. She gave me a big smile and a wave over her shoulder as they walked away.

As the girls, Bryan and I all got into our car, Bryan asked, "Who was that, Mrs. R?"

I caught the smitten tone in his voice and retorted, "A widow who's not ready to date, if that's what you're asking. Besides, she's 23. How old are you again?"

Bryan smirked. "Mentally, I'm 30, but really, I'm only 26."

I had never thought to ask how old he was before. He did act a lot older and seemed older because of his mustache and hairy features. So, I made a teasing remark to lighten the mood: "Oh, I couldn't tell with that mustache. You seemed to be, like... 36."

Bryan laughed and said that was the reason he grew it in the first place. He had a baby face underneath.

Lily chimed in, "Why don't you shave it?"

He patted Lily on the shoulder and smiled at her. "Well, you girls have given me a lot to think about tonight. Maybe I will..."

As we drove toward his dorm, I chimed to Lily "Don't take off your jacket, we still have to go to Lowe's so we can find someone to fix our garage". Bryan quickly asked, "What's wrong with your garage?"

I had told him that either the cold weather or Becca's driving must have loosened the chain for the motor.

Bryan responded that he knows which part I'd needed if I showed him the model and brand, so he asked "If you do find the right one, who's going to install it for you?"

I laughed. "Well, me, of course, who else? I'm going to try, at least..."

Bryan raised his eyebrows and asserted, "You need a professional for that. They can be tricky. If you want, I can come over and take a look at it and see if it can maybe be fixed before buying a new one...?"

I hadn't even thought about that option, but I didn't want to bother him. I internally sighed and was reminded that it was selfish of me to try and take the blessing of helping away from others because of my own pride. So, I said, "Thank you, Bryan. That sounds great. When are you available? And how about we make it a lunch afterwards?"

I realized 26-year-olds are younglings, and with him being broke, he could probably use a free home-cooked meal. He said that Saturdays or Sundays worked, so I chose Sunday since we all would already be at the service.

CHAPTER 19
~ Women Warriors ~

<u>Joanna</u>

On Sunday Morning, I woke up early to put the roast in the crockpot along with some potatoes and sweet carrots so that the meal would be ready by the time we all got back from the chapel.

We were running a bit late, but Becca was already waiting in the car. When a teenager gets to drive, suddenly they're always "on time".

I was a bit embarrassed that we arrived late to church, so we chose to sit in the last pew. I scanned the rows, hoping to see Jennifer Nunes, but there was no sight of her.

I did my best to focus on the worship and service. But I was a bit worried about Jennifer. Finally, I spotted her near the front. I made a mental note to make sure to speak with her after the service.

As the benediction proceeded, I noticed Bryan was 2 pews in front of Jennifer. He never turned around to look behind him, and he was attentive to the sermon... and so was she. My mind couldn't help but meander a bit, and I wondered if maybe they would be a good match for each other. I quickly shook my head to refocus on the sermon.

*****

As the service wrapped up, Jennifer was the one to find me in the crowd, and we all talked for a few minutes before Bryan showed up. He politely said hello to us all, and then stood back a step or two and graciously waited for us to finish chatting.

As Jennifer left, she waved goodbye to the girls, and then, as she was walking by Bryan, she added, "It was nice seeing you again." I caught the same gleam in her eye that I had seen in his, the Wednesday before when they had first met. I did my best to snap him out of it and said a little too loudly, "Ready to go? Ready for lunch?!" And, Bryan laughed at me.

As we drove back to our home, Bryan began to talk about his summer plans and his desire to go on a mission trip to South America and contribute on a worship team needed for a revival.

Proud and stunned, I encouraged, "That is wonderful, Bryan! It truly is. When you give and dedicate time to God, so intensely and altruistically, He will bless you. When is the trip?"

He replied, "I believe it's the first week of July."

"I'll make sure we do something special before you head out," I suggested. Jordan should be back by early June."

As we arrived home, we all got out of the car, and Bryan made a beeline for the garage door, as if that was priority. I turned around and said, "What are you doing, silly? We're eating first! I'm starving! Worry about that later..."

He smiled and humbly accepted, following us inside. The house smelled wonderful.

Becca and Lily set the table, and as they sat down to eat, the girls begin to poke fun at Bryan for not even having a bike. He reasoned that walking was the best way to elongate longevity in age.

The conversation briefly turned serious as Bryan talked about what a nice home-cooked meal it was that I had made for him and about how he had been praying that God would bless him with a wife and home of his own someday. More and more, he was starting to see that there were actually Devout women out there, and he had been praying that God would put just the right one in his path at the right time.

Bryan was grateful for the wonderful food and was honored to have been invited by the "chaplain's wife". He finished and immediately excused himself to look at the garage motor and all its components to see what was going on.

After only a few, short minutes, he had fixed the chain and the garage door. I couldn't believe it. I was so grateful. I asked him if I could pay him, and of course, he refused payment.

As he excused himself to use the bathroom, I quickly murmured to the girls, "Don't go change out of your church clothes and get comfortable just yet, we need to take Bryan home in a few minutes.

Becca was slightly annoyed and questioned, "Why can't you just take him, and I can stay home with Lily?"

I raised one eyebrow and did my best to give her the "mom" look. In a motherly tone, I answered, "First of all, because I'm your mother and I said so. Secondly, because it isn't ethical for me, as a married woman, to be alone with an unmarried man. One should never give people a reason to gossip." Becca wasn't pleased, but her attitude swiftly changed when she was given the opportunity to drive.

As Bryan came out of the restroom, he mentioned that he should probably get back to his dorm and study. He asked me to quickly try out the garage opener to see if it worked, and it sure did!

We all loaded back into the car to head back to base to drop him off. During the drive, he reiterated how thankful he was for the lunch and the leftovers I had packed for him to eat later.

As he walked towards his dorm and waved goodbye, I let my thoughts slip out loud to the girls, "He is a good kid. I pray he finds a great woman for a wife."

Lily interjected, "Like Ms. Jennifer?"

As usual, when I didn't know what to say, I answered her question with a question in order to get more information. "So why would you say Ms. Jennifer would be a good fit for Bryan?"

Lily tried to look through the rear-view mirror and get Becca's attention but couldn't, so she had no choice but to divulge and throw her sister under the bus. "Because Becca said they'd make a cute couple."

I now looked at Becca. "Ah, I see. I thought you were too busy with your schoolwork to pay attention to such things," I teased.

Becca, on the defense, answered, "I couldn't help overhear you talk about it with Dad. Plus, Mom, I can connect the dots. Besides, don't you think they'd be good together?

I shook my head and explained, "Girls, these two people, although they are good and genuine, need time to heal and get better from their past afflictions to move on. You know what Ms. Nunes went through, so we want to show and help her see that there is more to life, that she can be an independent mother and get back on her feet. That's why we've been seeing her a lot."

I paused to see if they were still listening. "Bryan is also getting back on his feet after that tremulous breakup. He was left with nothing. Now, we're showing him that there are still good women out there. By helping him, driving him to his dorm, and feeding him, we're showing acts of kindness and self-less love. Instead of Daddy preaching that to them, we're showing these two, in our actions, not just our words, how to understand God's love through us."

I could sense that I was losing my audience, so I decided to wrap it up by thanking them. "Thank you, girls, for being supportive and helping me keep busy. I know you guys miss, Daddy. I'm sure school has helped to distract your minds a bit, while I'm at home trying to figure a few things out, but I know it's hard. So, thank you, and I'm proud of both of you."

I decided it was best to end it like that, and I turned on the radio to Becca's favorite radio station to maintain a pleasant ambiance and end on a good note.

When we returned home, Bryan had left a ghostly imprint of what had been missing in our home: a manly figure—someone to fix things, help out around the house, appreciate good cooking, laughing with the girls...

As soon as we entered the house, Lily whispered, "I do miss Daddy."

Becca mumbled, "Yah, me too." On the last word, her voice cracked a little, and knowing that her big sister was sad too. Lily began to cry. I couldn't help it. I began to tear up as well as I tried to console Lily.

We all stood there for a bit, hugging each other in the front hallway. That moment helped us fortify our relationship as a better stronghold and brought us closer. We were three women warriors... ready for our king to come back home.

CHAPTER 20
~ Contagious Kindness ~

<u>Jordan</u>

While at Balad Air Base, I had time to renew my strength from God on a daily basis, as many Airmen came to me for emotional aid, advice, prayers, gatherings, etc.

Most of my frustration came from attempting to check emails. The U.S. Air Force was known for being the most powerful air force in the world; master of air, space, and cyberspace; and the most technologically advanced. However, ironically, the three things it failed to do properly were: deliver cargo on time, get aircraft satellite radios to work, and (the most frustrating of them all) have a working computer network on base.

When I did actually get it to work, I received the necessary peace of stability, prayer, love, and support from Joanna's emails—along with the letters that made me smile from the girls.

Every day, kindness was spreading throughout the unit, contagiously. Additionally, all three of my chapel services had exponentially grown in number.

My days were filled with activities, compromises, meetings, counseling, and so much more, and they all made the days go by really quickly.

Recently, I had been making it an objective to befriend Sergeant Crimson, since I had a strong heart tug from God to do so. We became friends quickly, and I felt like I had known him for years. There was something about him that reminded me of someone, but I couldn't quite figure who. His mannerisms and his aptitude to lead and help others seemed akin to a façade for something else, like he was trying to prove himself. It was eerily similar to a homebound character.

After a few weeks of spending time together, I managed to finally get Sergeant Crimson to tell me his back story after watching a movie during one of our breaks. Of course, I've found that it's over dinner when people are most vulnerable and able to talk about their personal history, so I kind of had the potential opportunity in the back of my mind.

I began with this question: "So... are you an only child? Married? Tell me a little bit about yourself."

He replied that he was an only child, had multiple failed relationships, and was currently single.

I continued to probe, "How about your parents? Are they together?"

Crimson took a deep breath, as if he wished I hadn't asked. He rasped out, "They're not together." He chewed a bite of his Philly cheesesteak for a bit, and I patiently waited for him to continue. "Haven't talked to either of them in years."

In an attempt to divert the attention off himself, he asked me, "Did you always wanted to be a chaplain?"

I smiled and responded, "No, I actually wanted to become an astronaut... or a pharmacist. I love chemistry and physics—science as a whole, really. However, I detest heights and flying, so I studied biochemistry in college."

As I swallowed a big bite of my own sandwich, I chuckled. "Then I heard from God that my career goal was not His plan for me, that I needed to pursue an education in theology, and trust in Him. So, I did, but I couldn't fathom what God wanted me to become. The day of graduation, I was approached by an Air Force chaplain from my church, and he invited me to lunch... and it all goes from there.

"Never had I thought I'd become a pastor, for I hated public speaking, embracing people, and socializing. But once I let God guide me, He began transforming me into His mold and began working on my flaws. Now I love what I do. I can publicly speak with my eyes closed, befriend a stranger, and still be the pharmacist... in my own household." That time he chuckled with me.

We talked for about an hour—about what his goals were, his spiritual state, etc. I tried to fish again about his parents, regarding their occupation and where they lived, and he shortly replied that he had "no idea where they were or what they were up to".

So, that led me to ask, "Are you upset at your parents?"

He didn't look up, stayed silent for an elongated five seconds, and finally said, "My parents failed me. I really don't want anything to do with them. I was raised by my mother."

With unbending persistence, I prodded, "Why are you upset with your mother?"

Again, he refused to give me eye contact and said, "I don't really know why..."

I knew he didn't want to divulge that information yet. This was the line, and I didn't want to cross it, so I changed the subject. "Well, it's getting late. We should probably head to bed."

He nodded as we both began to clean our respective trays and seating area.

As invigorated as I was, I missed my family immensely. Every morning and night, I made sure to dedicate a distinct prayer for the girls and Joanna. Strength, patience, comfort, wisdom—you name it. I prayed that He would bless my girls and keep them safe.

Joanna wrote me almost every day—loving and encouraging words that rejuvenated my spirit. If she only knew that just thinking of her was the reason I smiled here while at war. I tried to read her emails before I went to bed, in order to dissolve all the stress accumulated from the day.

Things were getting pretty intense here. Our briefs had increased regarding a surge in IDFs (indirect fire). I wished I could share with Joanna all the things I had seen or had happened, but I didn't want to worry her. I needed her prayers, support, encouragement, and to be as cheery as possible.

CHAPTER 21

~ Streams in the Desert ~

<u>Jordan</u>

As I was shutting down my computer and getting ready to leave the office, I heard a knock on my door. Captain Higgins opened the door slightly and peeked his head around it.

"Hello, sir, may I come in?" He arrived with a radiant aura that felt congruent to mine.

I said, "Of course, how are you?"

He didn't sit, but rather leaned against the armrest of the couch. He seemed to have news to tell me that he was building up to, but instead responded, "I'm doing great, sir. How about yourself?"

I responded the same and asked what I could do for him. He explained that even though he had not read the whole Bible, he felt an urge to get baptized and wanted me to baptize him in accordance with what the Scriptures instructed believers to do.

I was initially stunned at his request, because of what he went through, what he was doing now, and where we were. It had slipped my mind that God's will could be done anywhere, anytime. Happily, I accepted and discussed the whereabouts of the ceremony.

It was going to be a pretty tricky baptism. In the middle of a desert, in the driest possible place, surrounded by mountains... Additionally, we didn't have a tub in our chapel. Where would I immerse him? I knew who to ask: Sergeant Crimson.

*****

The next day I met with Crimson to ask him if he knew how we could build some kind of large container or if he was aware of an unused vessel since he was the head of security forces. Successfully, he showed me a large hole they had dug behind a building years ago for exercise and to practice physical training. It was the perfect solution for my inquiry.

I extended the invitation to Crimson if he wanted to come and support a member get baptized. I didn't really expect him to show up, since it was probably on his day off. I was just ecstatic that in the midst of war, someone had decided to focus on God and publicly decree his proclamation.

*****

As morning neared, I woke up to the sound of marching footsteps near my tent, much louder than usual. I laid on my bed, thinking of today's ceremonial water baptism, and I begin to ask God for His glory to emanate, His presence be known, and His will to be done. I sat up and began to get dressed. I decided to wear my silver necklace with a cross on it. It dangled perfectly alongside my dog-tags.

Suddenly, I heard a knock on my door, and I hollered, "Come in!"

It was Sergeant Crimson. "Good morning, Chaplain. I got everything ready for you. There are barrels full of warm water on my truck."

I was surprised. "Thank you, Sergeant! I was going to pick everything up on my way. You didn't have to do that, but I am so grateful!"

He responded that it wasn't a problem and that he was glad to be of help. It was his day off. I knew he could have been somewhere else, but for some reason, he was seeking me out. So, I took the opportunity for a quick morning talk about his family.

Somehow, he finally opened up...

"I was raised by a single mother. In a way, I've been angry at her for leaving my father when I was 8 years old. She prohibited me from contacting him. When I turned 18, she finally admitted he was an alcoholic-drug dealer and didn't want us around that environment. I was even more furious at her because I thought, *Why didn't you get him help?* So, I decided to look for him. I called my grandmother to obtain his whereabouts.

"He had died a year before I turned 18 from a lung disease. I was broken, enraged, resentful—you name it. I could have helped my father if she had allowed me to keep in touch with him. Who knows, he may have gone off the deep end because she took me away from him.

"That's why I joined the Air Force: to be around guys and learn to be a man. Now, I don't hate her, but I just don't want anything to do with her."

I began to lament his father's loss and discussed with him that it was his father's choices, and his only, that resulted in the consequences of his terminal illness. His death couldn't be blamed on anyone else. Secondly, I explained that his mother was trying to do the right thing at that time, and in her mind, it was the best choice for him. I also asserted that no parent was perfect. Food, shelter, safety, love... even if she wasn't perfect, she did provide that for him.

I decided to open up about my personal upbringing, as well, and how I, too, was raised by a single mother, along with my two siblings. I had to share a room with two siblings and a bed with my brother. However, that was the past, and for me to be happy, I needed to look beyond that forgive and forget (as much as I could).

He asked how he could get rid of all that pain and see his mother differently. I told him about Corporal Nunes and how everything worked out so that because of that tragedy, I was able to have off Thanksgiving week and be there for my mother when she was ill. Sometimes tragedy prepares you for various outcomes, and in pain, one gains strength.

I explained that I wished I could have done more to save Nunes, but ultimately, it was his choice. I had to do my best to see the positive and that at least two lives were spared. Finally, I shared the truth and gave credit to God. I shared with him that God's love was overflowing. It was so potent, it left no room for bitterness or resentment.

"Forgiving is one of God's commandments, you know?" I said.

Crimson mused, "I've heard that. There are just so many commandments—too many to follow and keep up with, sometimes, like harsh regulations. If it could be condensed into one, what would it be? And why did He impose so many?"

Without hesitation, I replied, "Matthew 22:37 is the verse to read. God really has one monumental commandment: 'You must love the Lord your God with all your heart, all your soul, and all your mind.' That is His first and greatest commandment. The reason God gave us bullet pointed commandments is because we needed them to be that way. We are humans. We are flawed, and our innate tendency is to be selfish. Love is selfless, and so God teaches us in detailed verses what selfless love is.

"For example, let's go over and summarize the Ten Commandments... when you love God with all of you, you have no room to have another God or idol. When you love God with all of you, you wouldn't blurt out His name in vain. Fearing Him, you would honor His request of making Sunday a holy day. When you love Him, you're full of divine love to respect and honor your parents in return, because He gave them to you, regardless of how flawed they are. When you love God, you wouldn't commit adultery or lie over tangible items, and you would love your neighbor enough to respect him.

"God's love should be centric to your life, and it will promote righteousness living. We have to fight and cleanse our human desires and habits. That's why, in a humorous way, God compares us to sheep. Sheep are incredibly dull and dumb. Psalm 100:3 says, 'Know that the Lord, he is God! It is he who made us, and we are his; we are his people, and the sheep of his pasture'.

"Another is Isaiah 53:6: 'All we like sheep have gone astray; we have turned, everyone, to his own way; and the Lord has laid on him the iniquity of us all.'

"And, in Jeremiah 50:6, He blatantly says, 'My people have been lost sheep...'

"Sheep are very unintelligent animals. They panic at an instance, have poor depth perception, and according to studies, are behind swine and cattle in brain activity. A sheep could drown in a riverbank because it has no common sense to retreat to the shallow edge.

"However, they have great memory and facial recognition. They have all five cognitive senses like we do; touch, smell, hearing, vision and taste. If we are like sheep, we are to follow Him for He leads us and has the senses to do so. Yet, we are doltish; we have the capability to recognize our Shepherd's voice.

"So that's why God had given Moses the Ten Commandments, but I think God was frustrated at how we failed consistently and eventually said, 'You know what, just love and follow me'."

I chuckled then, and so did Sergeant Crimson. "The extraordinary and marvelous part is that He loves me and you unconditionally."

I paused, gave him time to think, and watched his reaction to all I had said. I thought this was probably a good stopping point. I didn't want to overwhelm him either. Better to demonstrate with actions than words. Plus, I should probably eat breakfast. It felt like I had preached a Sunday sermon, and I didn't want to be late for my first deployment baptism in the desert.

CHAPTER 22
~ Believer's Baptism ~

Jordan

As we left the Chow Hall, we got into the truck full of barrels and slowly drove half the mile to our destination. Approaching the back strip of our "gym", I saw Captain Higgins already there along with some of his comrades.

Crimson backed up the truck, as I placed the plastic tarp in the hole in order to avoid mudding. The guys attending volunteered to assist by pulling all 4 corners of the tarp tight and holding them down with stakes. Then, they helped pour the barrels of water onto the tarp, creating a mini-pool, just deep enough to fully immerse Captain Higgins in.

I looked at Captain Higgins, and he was ready. He was eager to proclaim his faith and follow God. He neared me, and I quickly told him to take off his uniform. Then, I whispered, "Are you ready?"

He nodded with a smile and said, "Oh, yes, sir!"

As I began to step into the hole, I looked around at the multitude of service members surrounding us—sixty to eighty Airmen begin to clap. I couldn't believe that so many were in attendance. I gathered my Bible and began to speak.

I cleared my throat and did my best to project my voice so that all could hear. "Good morning, everyone!"

A slew of them replied back with variations of, "Good morning, sir/chaplain..."

I continued, "We are gathered here today to witness Captain Higgins profess his faith in Jesus. Now, some of you may be wondering why we do water baptism. It is because it is symbolic; it represents Christ rising from the dead. Hence, we are made new when we accept Him in our hearts."

I looked at Captain Higgins and gave him the nonverbal cue to go ahead and join me. He slowly stepped in, one foot at a time.

"Now, I'd like to begin with a prayer..." I scanned the crowd quickly to see if there were any objections, but one by one the men bowed their heads and waited for me to continue. I placed my hand on Captain Higgins' shoulder and prayed, "Lord Heavenly Father, You are good. You are the sovereign King, and we praise and worship You. Thank You for Your endless love.

"We come together before You to present Captain Higgins, as he is dedicating his life to You and becomes new, and we are asking that Your Holy Spirit dwell in him. In Your holy name we pray. Amen."

I resumed, "Captain Higgins, please repeat after me this confession: I believe that Jesus is the Christ... the Son of the living God...and I accept Him as my Lord and Savior...."

As I spoke each phrase and Captain Higgins repeated after me, the emotion and authenticity in his voice rang out clearly.

I placed my left hand on his right shoulder and my right hand on his forehead. I looked at him, then up to the skies. "Captain Higgins, I now baptize you in the name of the Father, the Son, and the Holy Spirit, for the forgiveness of your sins and the gift of the Holy Spirit."

Captain Higgins plugged his nose with his hands, took a deep breath, and closed his eyes. I dunked him wholly, immersing him fully in the water, and then I helped him come back up. The crowd erupted then with clapping and cheering. Many shouted "Amen" joyfully. We hugged, and I turned to him and said, "By faith, you are a saved man! Congratulations!"

Captain Higgins' commander and a few men from his squadron approached him with his towel. He then began to exchange hugs, hand slaps, and affirmations.

I picked up my towel and dried off. Several of the men volunteered to help dispose of the water and evacuate all the items around. Lieutenant Colonel Ferry approached me, gave me a firm handshake, and nonverbally nodded his approval with a big smile on his face.

*****

The next morning, I tried to catch Sergeant Crimson for breakfast before he started his shift. I thought that I had arrived early, so I slowly went down the line and took my time picking out my breakfast items. I brewed my coffee. I toasted my toast. I mixed the pancake batter and poured it on the girdle. I refilled my orange juice... twice.

I baited Crimson with two empty seats next to me, hoping he'd bite. I was starting to lose hope of his arrival. I conceded waiting for him, so I began to eat my breakfast. The third bite in, I felt a tap on my shoulder.

As I'm chewing, Crimson asked, "Mind if I sit here, sir?"

I chewed quickly and swallowed. "No, please, have a seat!" I looked over to see that he didn't have a tray. Instead, he accommodated himself and postured his hands in a prayer stance, while avoiding making eye contact with me.

Slightly confused, I asked, "Everything ok?"

He shook his head and said, "Thank you for inviting me to yesterday's event. I was left stunned... and ashamed. I realized how much bitterness and hatred I have held in my heart just from looking at Captain Higgins. I want what he has. I mean, I remember him months ago. He was the typical jock boy with that cocky attitude..."

I interrupted, "You can't give what you don't have. It was love. Love transformed him, and it directly generates from God. Like I said before, you can have it too."

He refused to look at me. Maybe from shame? I could see a tear running down his cheek. I felt a barrier come down between us. He realized he was held in bondage by hatred and deception.

He plead, "Sir, I don't know what to do... and right now, I have to go, but would you mind praying for me?"

"Of course not! I would love to!" I moved my breakfast tray to the side, turned my chair towards him, and laid my right hand on his shoulder.

We both closed our eyes, and I began to pray, "Dear Heavenly Father, I bring forth to you this young man, Darren Crimson. Lord, You know what he's been through, what he's dealt with, and what his future is planned out to be. He's at a moment right now where he needs You. Reveal Yourself to him, Father. Please, show him the everlasting and unconditional love that only You can offer. Take these heavy burdens he's been carrying for years and replace them with your peace that surpasses understanding.

"Jesus, You tell us that You are the Son, our King, but also our Friend. Please guide Darren towards a relationship with You, and transform him into a new creature.

"We pray this prayer in faith, in the name of the Father, the Son, and the Holy Spirit. Amen."

I knew he was in a rush, but I wanted to be sure he heard the confidence of hope I had, the loving tone, and the tenacity of praying in faith. As I opened my eyes, I found his face full of emotion, and he said, "Thank you, Chaplain. I appreciate the prayer."

He got up and left. I turned back around towards my tray and resumed the prayer in my head... *God, open his heart and let the seed of hope, faith, and love grow. Demonstrate Yourself and let him find You in many ways he couldn't before.*

I was dismayed that I hadn't invited him to the services, but I knew it was the Holy Spirit guiding my words. I didn't want to push too much on him. Besides, he knew when and where the services were held. He needed to come on his own, not because of guilt or pressure.

Well, God had a comical way of showing His works just at the right time in the right place, sometime when I was least expecting it. I knew it was His way of keeping me on my toes.

CHAPTER 23
~ Buyer's Remorse ~

Jordan

Weeks passed by, and I was glad to say Crimson had been attending the services when he was able to. I hadn't been able to spend as much as time with him as we had before, because I had been busier with briefings, field exercises, and conducting assistance with special operations. He did pass by a couple days ago to let me know he decided to write to his mom—the same day Joanna emailed me to let me know she was going on a cruise with the girls.

It was kind of a perfect timing, as I was commissioned to a two-day secret operation with a unit. I wouldn't be able to communicate with Joanna and she wouldn't have much access to communication either. I didn't want to worry her, so I just told her to have fun with the girls and that I missed them and loved them very much. I was so proud of them for staying busy, socializing, and congregating with our military family.

Joanna had always been independent, and long deployments and short TDY's sure had made her stronger, but she was quick to mention in her last letter that there was much I was still needed around for.

I smiled at the thought. I couldn't stop laughing when she sent me a picture of our front lawn as she tried to mow it. Let's just say landscape is not her forte. She mentioned that Bryan had been volunteering after church services to help out when necessary in return for a home-cooked meal. From what Joanna told me, helping around their home had been a positive edification process for him.

I was so grateful that she continued to be my advocate when I couldn't be there. I had planted seeds by preaching before I had left, and now Joanna was helping those seeds to grow and helping me fulfill God's intended purpose. Some reaped for others to sow. She made me feel so proud, yet at the same time subpar at how a wondrous woman like that could love me. It was an ever-daily reminder of how God loves us, never keeping track of our past.

*****

Later that same day, I had a young Airman in her early thirty's come into my office for advice. She explained that her husband was upset she was writing and/or talking more to their kids than him. She said she obviously loves him and that he's over-reacting and being immature. The kids needed to hear from her because they are children and her husband should know better. She wanted to be a good parent and a good wife, as she already felt horrible that she had to be away.

As I sat and listened, I had to explain that although their children missed mommy, children's love would be satisfied knowing that mom and dad were doing great. A frustrated father without the words or support of his wife could deteriorate his spirit and slowly cede his role as the father-figure.

A good marriage could produce good parenting, but good parenting couldn't produce a good marriage. I had to let this young woman know that women could do all things men could, but not the other way around. Women have more patience, tender care, multi-tasking skills, better listening skills, and are usually the domestic goddesses that are prevalent in the daily home functions.

To give her a better example, I told her that I spoke and wrote to my wife first, and if I had time, I would connect with the girls. The girls needed their mom to be strong. She and I had a mutualistic relationship. By feeding off each other, we helped each other to better ourselves.

When one is ready to marry, they must understand that it's a contractual agreement with three parties—the husband, the wife, and God. Marriage licenses never expire, and the marriage bond required daily maintenance and practice to grow stronger.

After five weeks, that young woman came back to thank me. Things were improving greatly. Their kids rarely needed to hear from her, and her husband felt more emotionally secure.

*****

I woke up just before my alarm clock went off. I knew today was going to be a day. I had to accompany two convoys that would be meeting with another unit in the desert to trade supplies with an NGO (Non-governmental organization). The NGO could not meet us at our post, since they had been declared as a neutral party in this war arena. They tended to avoid conflict-of-interest or foreign invasions. To prove their declared state of neutrality, they required a peaceful transaction, and in order to assure that, they requested that at least one chaplain be in attendance.

I completed my ritual morning prayer, ate breakfast, and packed all my things for the two-day operation. It was about a four-hour drive that would be prolonged by many cautious stops, bathroom breaks, and ground-call reports. Then, we would camp to wait for the contractor to arrive, talk, inspect, trade, verify, and load up the cargo.

I walked over to the hangar to meet there with two NCO's (noncommissioned officers), an Airman, and the Communications Intelligence Field Officer, Major Ajkhi.

Major Ajkhi was a born native from Uzbekistan that was rescued in the early 1990's as a child from a terrorist cell. He had dedicated his life to helping the United States in foreign relations with various Middle Eastern countries.

Once I arrived at the hangar, I looked around to see who we were missing. It seemed Sergeant O'Hara hadn't yet arrived. Yesterday, he showed up late at the briefing because he was not feeling well. I hoped he was alright because we really needed him; this was to be a five-man operation.

I decided to use the restroom quickly before I boarded the Humvee, so I placed my bag in the backseat and closed the door. I had used the restroom before getting here, so I knew it was nerves getting to me. Nonetheless, I did have to pee (again). As I came out, I saw everyone already loaded up on the first vehicle. I was to ride on the second Humvee with Senior Airman Velasquez. I slid onto the backseat, and he turned to ask, "Hello, sir! Ready?"

I nodded. No one was really ever "ready" to drive in the middle of the desert. I tried to review the mission's briefing in my mind and recall all important key points of the expedition.

I asked Sergeant Velasquez who the lead driver was, and to my surprise, he answered that it was Sergeant Crimson. My nerves suddenly became ebullient to know that I had a friend with me.

Velasquez injected, "Yeah, I think Sergeant O'Hara got food poisoning or some sort of stomach virus, so Crimson volunteered."

"Ah, ok, gotcha." I slowly nodded and paused for about ten seconds and then requested, "Do you mind if I pray for us?"

He shook his head. "No, sir. Please do. We need all the help we can get."

Although he had his eyes open to drive us out, he earnestly looked back at me to assert reverence to the best of his ability. I, on other hand, bowed my head and closed my eyes...

"Dear Lord, we come before You to say thanks. Thank You for a beautiful day. In the midst of everything, You are with us. I humbly ask that You send angels to watch over us, protect us, and give us the ability to complete this mission safely. We ask in Your name. Amen."

I wanted to make sure it was a quick, straight-to-the-point prayer before we left the gates. Drivers needed to be fully attentive of surroundings and retain the ability to listen to the radio for important communications.

As we got clearance to head out through the east gate, Sergeant Velasquez and I began to listen for radio calls within the first half hour. Major Ajkhi spoke to our team about the coordinates we needed to meet to feel "safe".

For a few minutes, my mind drifted away, and I began to think my life over—my marriage, my career, my whole life... It was such a reminiscent feeling. Embarking into an unknown territory, you begin to think of the known, your past, memories. I quickly snapped out of it as Sergeant Velasquez struck up a conversation by asking me about my background and my family.

We started talking about where we were from, where we were both stationed, our families, etc. He was quite a bit more diverse than the other Airmen I'd spoken to. His family was from Costa Rica and came to the States to pursue better opportunities for themselves.

Velasquez grew up in Dubuque, Iowa to attract Stateline customers to his parent's restaurant. Hence, he'd been Americanized at a young age. He felt the need to serve and give back to the United States, because this country fulfilled the American dream for his family. He had a son and another one on the way, and he was hoping to be back before his wife was due to give birth. I found him to be a merry, cordial young man.

*****

As we're about to the halfway point of our destination, we heard on the radio from Major Ajkhi that Captain McKenzie was requesting that we pull over. She needed a bathroom break.

I watched as both Humvees slowly pulled over, and Sergeant Crimson and Velasquez did a quick check around to ensure a safe stop. It looked pretty safe, with miles and miles of sand, and no questionable terrain in sight.

Because of that, we were all sure to look away from Captain McKenzie and give her privacy to relieve herself. She walked by us and knocked on our door to signal "ready", and then continued to get in her vehicle.

After another two hours, we arrived at our destination: a small camp with various flags. As we approached the gate, we showed our badges to the guards. We trailed the lead as we parked our Humvees in a parallel formation in case negotiations went awry and we needed to leave quickly. I grabbed my backpack and put it on as I stepped out of the vehicle.

Crimson hollered at me to follow him, and we made our way inside a shack. Major Ajkhi held the door for all of us to get inside, closed it, and then announced, "Alright, looks like we're here a bit early, so let's eat!"

We all reached in our bags and pulled out sandwiches, chips, and goodies to munch on. We all packed MRE's (meals ready to eat) in case of emergency, but for now, we were able to eat decent food.

We all began to unwind a bit, and I sat back and poked fun at Crimson. "You just couldn't let it go. You drove 4 hours, AND into a different time zone, to follow me, just to get another whoopin'?" I was referring to the card game Uno, we had been playing almost every other night and that I had just noticed he had brought along in his backpack.

He snickered and gave me the side eye. He seemed in good spirits, but something seemed different. He uttered while chewing, "My mom responded to my letter... I thought she'd be mad, but I was wrong. Her letter was lighthearted, and she asked me to forgive her."

As he swallowed, I responded, "Wow, that's awesome, man. I'm so glad! So, you were able to find her, huh? Where is she living now?"

He looked up and was about to answer, but then, he quickly got cut off.

"Hey, guys, COMSA is here," Captain McKenzie interjected, as we all finished eating. COMSA, a Turkish company with a branch in Iraq, manufactured parts for various weapons, including ammunition, air defense artillery, and tanks. While the DoD preferred to buy parts from companies, such as Lockheed and General Dynamics, sometimes the turnaround to get special parts made took too long and had too high a cost. Sometimes, it was just easier to get what we needed from local sources.

We all grabbed our things and headed out towards the meeting place—some big building across from us. Major Ajkhi led the way, Velasquez followed, then me and McKenzie, and then Crimson.

We all entered the old, rugged, cement building that had lots of lighting everywhere. Major Ajkhi began to introduce himself to the 3 men standing in the middle. I couldn't understand most of what he was saying, since he was speaking Arabic. I just nodded and shook their hands when we engaged eye contact.

Ajkhi and McKenzie sat down at the table before them and began to exchange files with two of the contractors. The third one seemed nervous, and he avoided eye contact with me as he shook my hand

and turned away. I decided to join Velasquez and Crimson, where they were hanging out by the door monitoring the area.

"Hey, guys…" I interrupted.

Velasquez, very watchful, looked back warily and whispered, "I don't have a good feeling about this…"

Behind me, I could hear the agreement going on and McKenzie standing up. She came up behind us and said, "Okay, gentlemen, we're done. We just gotta get the cargo."

I couldn't help but think that was seriously the fastest transaction I'd seen in my life. She stood with us, awaiting Major Ajkhi to join, as the other men follow. We scooted back, and allowed the men go before us and lead the way to their awning for the exchange.

The blazing hot sun forced all of us to speed walk in order to avoid its oppressing heat, amplifying the sound of our boots stepping on the stones. We arrived at the barricade they had anchored. Major Ajkhi asked them to unload the part, view its functionality, inspect it, and place it on our Humvee.

They seemed very cooperative and helpful, except that one man who continued to avoid eye contact. The hairs on my back began to spike, so I immediately commenced a quick prayer in my head. I knew I was being judged as an outsider because I was the chaplain.

I slowly took a few steps back, hoping to refrain from the "conversation circle" and fade out of sight.

As they strapped the cargo onto the Humvee, Velasquez did the finger circular motion to wrap things up, signaling we were set to go. I picked up my bag and headed towards the Humvee.

Major Ajkhi smiled and said, "See, Captain, that wasn't so bad."

I wasn't sure if he was talking to me, or McKenzie, since she was walking beside me. We all got into our respective vehicles and signaled to one another with thumbs up that we were ready to go.

I laughed in my mind because Velasquez was already seat belted with the vehicle turned on, and had his foot on the pedal, ready to speed out of here. Anxious as he was, he began to reverse and lead the way out of the camp, as Major Ajkhi, McKenzie, and Crimson followed behind us. As we drove by the contractors we just negotiated with, they all waved, except the one that seemed apprehensive, as he turned around and disappeared from eye's view.

CHAPTER 24
~ The Allegory of John ~

Jordan

As we turned the corner, I took a deep breath, exhaled, and I fully depleted of all the tension built-up in my body. An upsurge of peace was felt, as I sat back, relaxed my body, and dropped all of my belongings from my lap to the floor. I sensed the same release of tension from Velasquez as he spat his gum out the window. He sure wanted to get the out of there, which his speeding clearly displayed.

We began the return to our command post, heading back the same way we came. About fifteen minutes en route, we received a radio call from Major Ajkhi stating McKenzie needed to stop and relieve herself again.

Velasquez immediately murmured, "We haven't even left the outskirts... Can't she wait another 10 minutes?! Or utilize a pee bag?"

I immediately interjected, "We should stop. Major Ajkhi has strict religious beliefs; he would not feel comfortable having McKenzie just pee right next to him. It's impolite and embarrassing for both of them."

Velasquez shook his head. "Sir, this isn't a clear area. I can't see beyond those alleys…" He sighed as he looked around. "Okay, okay, I guess I'll pull over."

I couldn't imagine the struggles of female combat soldiers and what they had to deal with to use the restroom in times of war, missions, field training, etc. Velasquez parked on the road, but he didn't turn off the ignition.

McKenzie hollered and waved to our Humvee, "So sorry!"

Velasquez and I both surveyed our surroundings, and at almost the exact same time, we turned towards the other Humvee and heard a mild, shrill whistle. A sharp blast of dirt exploded on the left side of our vehicle.

I covered my ears, trying to get the ringing from the high-pitched soundwaves to stop. It was deafening. I yelled to Velasquez, "Go! Go! Go!"

With the stirred-up dirt and dust from the blast blinding us, there wasn't much that we could see, but Velasquez put the vehicle into gear and stepped on the gas anyways. As soon as we began to move, we heard a clank under our Humvee. My heart dropped; my respiratory system choked. In my mind, all I could do was cry out to God for help, as our Humvee was blasted by an IED that threw the vehicle into an upward jump. It landed on the driver side, knocking both Velasquez and I unconscious.

*****

I began regaining consciousness to the sound of bullets swooshing by.

Everything happened so quickly. McKenzie radioed in for help and back-up as she gave out the coordinates and status. Her voice was steady, but it was also filled with fear. Crimson, Ajkhi, and McKenzie already had their weapons out and were returning fire at the insurgents down the hill from where our Humvees had landed.

My eyes were open, but my body was still paralyzed in fear. It was if my mind had just given up and couldn't possibly process any additional information. I silently plead with the Lord to be with us and to get us out of this battle quickly and safely.

As I began to slowly move my neck, I lifted my hands, inspecting them, wiggling my fingers. It was so surreal. I felt like I had never seen my hands before. Suddenly, a sharp pain took my breath away, as shock started to gradually subside a bit. I looked down at my left leg. I was pretty sure I had at least sprained my knee, when the blast pushed me to the driver's side of the vehicle.

I unbuckled my seatbelt. I could still move it, but it sure hurt. I pulled myself forward and hovered over the front seat to check on Velasquez. He was still unconscious and had blood seeping from a deep gash in his neck. I placed my fingers just above the wound to check for a pulse. There was light pulsation.

I went to unbuckle Velasquez to be able to better assess his injuries. As I reached down to release his seatbelt, I could see that his right foot was completely bent and broken, twisted at a grotesque angle.

I had the quick flashback of how Velasquez probably meant to slam on the brake pedal but got it stuck once the Humvee flipped. I tried to wiggle Velasquez out of that trapped position. I detached a harness, wiggled up, and pulled him out toward the passenger seat, making sure our helmets were on tightly before attempting to get out.

I popped my head out of the passenger window to clear for any threats. I could see Major Ajkhi and Crimson both taking cover by their vehicle. Major Ajkhi spotted me and yelled, "Jordan, are you and Sarge' [Sergeant] alright?!"

I hollered back, "I'm alright! Velasquez is unconscious and has a severely broken foot. He needs medical attention!"

Major Ajkhi signaled for us to stay in the vehicle, as they maintained their defensive position and kept aiming towards the bushes.

I remembered that there was a medical kit on the back of the Humvee as well as my IFAK (Individual First Aid Kit). I took it out and unpacked the adhesive bandages, saline, and alcohol to sterilize the major cut on Velasquez's neck. I opened his vest to ensure no other critical wound was missed. There were no additional wounds that I could see.

As I was completing his injury assessment, I located Velasquez's weapon. Instinctually, I reached for it just in case I would be needing it for self-defense, then I stopped. I was confident with all the practice rounds I did in Texas I could take out anyone if I really needed to.

Ironically, a chaplain while in civilian status can protect himself rather in a combat zone. It's been a controversial topic over the years.

McKenzie took out the thermal optics to spot how many of them were out there. She scanned it twice to verify her count, and she yelled, "There are two of them 150 meters east!"

Crimson and Major Ajkhi aim toward the area McKenzie pointed and began to shoot until McKenzie yelled, "Target #1 down!"

Crimson then shot his last round, and McKenzie yelled, "Target #2 down! I repeat, both targets down!"

Major Ajkhi then yelled, "Cover!" for Crimson to keep on the lookout as Major Ajkhi ran over to out tilted Humvee. He did a quick check for gas leaks or other IED's.

Ajkhi popped his head in the passenger window and looked in at my handiwork of the bandaging I had done to Velasquez. With all my might, I quickly picked up Velasquez to pass him over to Major Ajkhi, who carefully pulled him out and put him on his shoulder.

Major Ajkhi looked back at me and asked, "Chaplain, you alright? You're bleeding on your leg..."

I hadn't noticed the blood before... I shook my head. "It's just a banged-up knee. It's fine for now..."

Ajkhi had gently laid Velasquez in the back. As soon as he laid him down, Velasquez began to hemorrhage from his neck. Ajkhi opened the first aid kit that had been stored in the back, and McKenzie unloaded all the contents of the bag for him. She began to hold pressure on his neck.

Ajkhi quickly put on gloves and picked up the heavy gauze and adhesive bandages. He took over holding the pressure firmly on Velasquez' neck, as he instructed McKenzie to open all the supplies. He then replaced the gauze with the heavy layered one and began to band aid him with the adhesive surgical tape. Then, Ajkhi instructed McKenzie to continue to radio for back-up as he checked for other injuries on Velasquez.

Vigilant, Crimson overheard the commotion going on with Ajkhi and McKenzie and decided to check in on me. "You alright, sir?"

I nodded as I finished bandaging up my knee and applying an ice pack. "Yeah, I may need help getting out of the vehicle, though."

Crimson reached his hand down to help me stand up and placed my arm around his neck for support. As soon as we stood up fully, we heard at a distance, heavy breathing. We both turned around to see Target #2. He was dirty, with blood all over, struggling to crawl, coming after them.

Crimson didn't seem overly concerned and continued to assist in helping me towards the other vehicle. He was confident he shot him good, bound to die soon...

We both continued to limp towards the other Humvee when we heard a faint, but distinctive sound: a pin lever clicked and clanked on the pavement. Target #2, with all his might had thrown a frag grenade towards us.

Everything happened then in less than a second. Crimson and I looked at each other with profound insight and understanding, recognizing our mutual respect. This was it. Peace flooded through my body as I closed my eyes and prepared to meet Jesus face to face.

Crimson didn't even hesitate. With all his might, I felt him lift me and push me far... at least 6 to 7 feet away behind the Humvee. I watched in horror as he threw his body over the grenade, shielding me from its blast and blowout debris. The frag detonated and Crimson exploded into a fine pink mist.

"No! No! No! Nooooooooo!" I screamed. "Gooooooood! NO!" I drug myself towards where the blast had occurred, my mind not comprehending that there was no way that Crimson could have survived. With unforeseen will, I was assaulted with the flashback of Nunes laying on the floor, blood pooling around his body... blood everywhere... so much blood.

In shock, I could not move. I could not blink. *Dear Lord, what just happened? Joanna. Think about Joanna. Get up. Move.* My thoughts and my body seemed disconnected, but somehow, with as much sanity as I could muster, I began to crawl back behind the Humvee as I heard bullets fly past me.

McKenzie had shot Target #2 down to ensure that he was no longer a threat. She ran toward me then, picked me up, placed my arm around her neck and drug me as we hobbled towards the back seat of the Humvee.

She sat me in the back and did a quick assessment. "Sir, you alright...!? Chaplain...!? JORDAN!?"

That got my attention, and I nodded with hesitation, grief-stricken. I looked down at my hands. Dirt mixed with blood made a brown clay-looking substance on my hands. I wiped them on my pants. Then, I became strangely upset that my pants were dirty. I began to shake violently.

McKenzie held onto my hands tightly then. "Chaplain, hey, you're in shock. You're okay. Shhhh…" She evaluated me fully and told me I was okay. No open wound except the scratches and cuts on my what turned out to be a broken knee.

She kept shushing me, like I child, and I couldn't figure out why. It took me a few minutes to realize that along with the uncontrollable shaking, I was also crying.

McKenzie switched places with Major Ajkhi to keep the pressure on Velasquez's neck, while Ajkhi ran with a blanket to collect what was left of Crimson's body.

McKenzie yelled at me, "Sir, I need your help! I need to drive us safely out of here, I need you to place your hands right here with full pressure!" She grabbed my hands and placed them on Velasquez's neck… fully sealed with medical tape. My hands stopped shaking then. Velasquez's life was literally in my hands. I began breathing heavily, deep cleansing breaths, and I closed my eyes to pray.

McKenzie jumped into the driver's seat and pedaled towards Major Ajkhi with Crimson's body. To avoid more trauma, Major Ajkhi placed the body in the back seat, behind them, so I could focus on Velasquez.

While McKenzie drove, Ajkhi kept a lookout for further attacks. McKenzie called to me, "Sir, you doing okay?! Be sure to put max pressure!"

I locked eyes with McKenzie in the rearview mirror, and a strange, warm peace washed over my body. I breathed in, breathed out, breathed in, breathed out, like the ocean's waves rhythmically hitting the shore. "I'm okay, McKenzie. Thank you. I'm okay…"

I began to pray then for Velasquez, supplicating that he would make it. *Please, God, spare his life.*

After driving about 10 minutes further, we heard a medevac helicopter approaching nearby. McKenzie radioed in to the pilot where she would be stopping so that he could land in clear sight. With agreed coordinates, the helicopter landed, and the rescue team jumped out with their equipment.

Major Ajkhi spoke with the lead medic and informed him of everyone's status, highest to lowest priority regarding their conditions. The lead medic jumped into the backseat to verify Ajkhi's assessment of Crimson as "deceased". Confirming his allegation, he rushed to the back to assess Velasquez, and yelled for the rest of the team to bring the gurney.

He took Velasquez's pulse, and confirmed that he was still alive, but needed immediate medical attention. They placed him on the litter and carried him back to the helicopter, as the rest of the team placed what was left of Crimson on the other litter. The second medic approached me and evaluated my cuts and agreed that my knee looked broken. Major Ajkhi gave the orders to take me in the helicopter too to ensure full evaluation and treatment in case they missed anything.

The full medical team began to clean and treat Velasquez, since he was determined to be in critical condition. I sat quietly in the back as they worked on the sergeant. I looked around, as if in a dream. I had never been in a helicopter before. As my eyes scanned the details of the helicopter's interior, my eyes landed on the body bag of Crimson's corpse.

A sudden wave of overwhelming grief crashed into me. I closed my eyes and begged and pleaded with God to have mercy on that young man's soul. He had given his life for me. John 15:12-13 flooded my mind:

> *12This is My commandment, that you love one another as I have loved you. 13There is no greater love than to lay down one's life for one's friends.*

I dropped my head, covered my face with my hands, and began to weep heavily.

*****

Once we arrived back at base, they wheeled Velasquez in immediately for an emergency surgical operation. A gurney was brought out for me to take me in and assess the extent of my knee injury. They also pronounced Crimson officially with a time of death.

*****

The doctor successfully was able to treat Velasquez with his mild head trauma and hemorrhage. For health progression, Velasquez and I were transported to Ramstein AFB Hospital in Germany for treatment and observation. Our families were notified of the incident, and they were told we would be returning home as soon as it was safe for us to travel.

Chapter 25

~ Soothing Aloe ~

<u>Jordan</u>

The first day back home, I didn't even have the motivation to feel excited. I had awoken many times in the middle of the night, unable to sleep, tossing and turning. It was possibly because of jetlag or my mind being overloaded.

I got up very carefully, slowly—ensuring that nothing would wake up Joanna. I walked towards my closet, swiftly grabbed the door knob, walked inside it, and gently closed the door. To have witnessed the gory and morbid death of two men in half a year was just too much to bear.

Unable to frame my thoughts, I disintegrated emotionally and collapsed on the closet floor. My extremities felt numb, yet an internal rampart of adrenaline inundated my central nervous system. I had reached my maximum capacity for mental and physical exertion. Sensibly, I had tried to bury one painful experience of seeing a stranger die, but adding the loss of Crimson, him giving his life for me, was just an incomprehensible amount of affliction. As much as I anticipated my homecoming and seeing the girls, I knew I wasn't ready to face them.

After a few minutes of ventilation, I decided to drug myself to sleep, with something strong and potent that would be sure to knock me out. I slowly snuck out of my closet, and I walked out of my bedroom towards the kitchen. I opened my medicinal cabinet and begin to look for my Ambien pills that I had been prescribed years ago when I had a cyst removed.

I had to get some sleep for tomorrow's interview. I call it an "interview", but we all knew it was an appointment with the mental health specialist to evaluate me.

I found the pills, took the prescribed amount, and went straight back to bed.

*****

As I woke up, I did my best to keep my eyes closed and sleep some more, but I knew that was it: time to move, make an effort. I turned to check on Joanna, and to my surprise, she was still in bed. So, I quietly rolled out of bed, slipped on my slippers, gently opened the bathroom door, and quietly shut it behind me.

I went about my business, brushed my teeth, and washed my face. I looked in the mirror and glanced at myself for a very long ten seconds. I looked beat. For the first time in a long time, I did not want to face another morning. I slowly opened the door to find that Joanna was no longer in bed.

I found her in the kitchen, cooking. I immediately stopped her, grabbed her hand, and led her to a seat at the table. I kissed her forehead and took over finishing the cooking for her. My body was on auto-pilot mode—time to do, not think.

As kind as she was to cook me breakfast, I didn't want to sit and think. I just needed to stay busy. She was quiet, meek; I could feel her psychoanalyzing me. I wanted to talk to her, but I didn't want to talk. As I flipped pancakes, I turned around and said, "I love you."

I turned on the radio to throw her off, signaling that I was okay, but that I just wanted peaceful music. I purposely made loud noises with the pots and pans, hoping to wake up the girls and have them come bring conversation to the table.

As I was setting up the plates on the table, there was a sudden bubbling pop that burst from the pan. I quickly rushed to flip the batter, and when I did, it disintegrated...

I broke down then, and I completely lost it. It had triggered imagery I was hoping to forsake. Sudden rage boiled through me. I threw the spatula across the kitchen and into the sink as I tried to contain myself, but it was inevitable. The tears began to stream down my face.

Joanna rushed to throw herself at me with a hug and began to cry with me. I wailed, "Why Joanna?! He... he was just a kid. I don't even know if he's in Heaven!"

She soothed my back with her hand and whispered, "Baby, he died because he was introduced to love. Loving others before himself. 'Greater love has no one than this...' God's Word says so."

The girls were by the stairs witnessing my break-down on the floor, watching and hoping that their mother could lift me up and restore me.

Becca pulled Lily's hand and signaled her to go back upstairs with her. Even with the lack of understanding, Becca knew that giving space was sometimes best for one to recover. However, Lily wouldn't budge. After a few minutes, Joanna signaled them to come over and give me a hug.

They all knew what disease I now had. I had worked with many other soldiers who had struggled with PTSD, but now, I was no longer in the audience. My family and I were the full cast and crew for this season of life's scene.

CHAPTER 26
~ Beneath the Surface ~

<u>Joanna</u>

I drove Jordan to the clinic for his formal psychological evaluation. I grabbed his hand as we waited in the parking lot and began to pray. He thanked me for my support and coming along.

As we both got out of the car, we walked together slowly, holding hands. We checked-in at the front desk.

When his name was called, I kissed his hand, reiterated how much I loved him, and assured him that I would be waiting for him.

While he was being evaluated, I walked outside the clinic and headed to the chapel, hoping to pray uninterrupted.

I saw the conference room light on and assumed everyone was in a meeting. I quickly walked into the sanctuary. I needed to be in the presence of God, to talk to Him, plead with Him... I could only do so much. It was the Lord that was going to heal Jordan's invisible and visible wounds.

I knew I had to sharpen myself and fortify for him, oversee the household for a while, until Jordan recovered from this disease. It would be temporary, but that's what marriage thrives on: teamwork.

My heart ached for Jordan, I could feel his grief. Never in my life did I imagine my best friend would be this hurt.

It's as if he's a punching bag, and life comes at him with gradual jabs.

I run towards the altar and I begin to weep with heavy emotions. I try to refrain from asking *God, why us? Why him?*

Within fighting my inner battle, I break down and just begin to thank God instead; for his life and safe return.

 I asked God for strength, wisdom, and guidance through everything that was going to come our way. I knew that we had barely scratched the surface of what we had yet to face.

CHAPTER 27
~ A Way in the Wilderness ~

Jordan

After a couple of days, I received a phone call from Sergeant Miller that Crimson's had mother requested to speak with me. I had 60 days of CTO (Compensatory Time Off) medical leave to spend time with my family, therapy for my PTSD (Post Traumatic Stress Disorder) and knee recovery. I was on strict orders not to over-stress, not to rush and get into work mode, and to take things day by day.

I had been devastated the whole month I was in Germany receiving treatment for my knee, thinking and praying of what I was going to say to Crimson's mother. Since he had told me that they had begun to speak and reconnect, I knew that the clock was ticking and that it was the right thing to speak with her.

I accepted to meet with her, both to tell her what a hero her son was and for my emotional closure. Just before hanging up the phone, I asked Sergeant Miller what her name was.

As Sergeant Miller's voice answered my question through the phone in what seemed like slow motion, my stomach churned upside down. I fell to my knees in disbelief. *No, dear God, please no!*

I ran to the bathroom before my emotions networked with my body organs to empty themselves of anything and everything that they were holding.

After I had finished vomiting, Joanna had heard the sudden anguish, and she ran to the bathroom doorway. "Honey, what's wrong?!" She fell to her knees and wrapped her arms around me.

I was wailing, hyperventilating, rocking back and forth on the bathroom floor. I stopped for a moment, took a deep breath in between my hiccupping sobs, and blurted out, "Blanca Wade. Crimson's mother is Blanca."

*****

As I woke up from the whirl of a night, I wanted to look my best for Ms. Blanca. I was nervous. I was hesitant, dreading the drive, wishing time would stop and swallow me. I had asked Joanna to drive me, and she agreed.

I was now regretting having agreed to meet with her. *What would I say? How would I approach her?* Because of me, she would now never again see her son.

For open wounds to heal, there would be setbacks, infections, inexplicable changes, unknown side effects... Regardless, I knew that I had to face and treat any sudden injuries, even though I felt ashamed and disgusted with myself. I just couldn't believe it. Every church member had a story and almost all of them had wished to share their stories with the chaplain. But, not Blanca. She had kept her book hidden. But now, I would be a part of her story forever, and she in mine.

*****

Joanna held my hand and began to pray for me on the way to base. She was God's gift and remedy for this time in my life... and all times, really. I could feel God's love through her—her compassion, grace, mercy, hope... the list went on and on... I blanked out on listening to her prayer, for I had my own prayer, voicing my gratitude and humility.

She showed her greatest strengths through moments of weakness and frailty, and what I loved the most was that she regenerated her strength from our Lord. I could see and feel it. I recognized that she was what made me whole. I loved her more than myself, and I would do anything to make her happy. Just like that, I felt utter peace.

She finished her prayer and said, "I'll be right here."

I smiled and respond, "I know." I winked at her and closed the door.

I took a deep breath and walked towards the entryway. Ms. Blanca was waiting for me in the chapel, sitting patiently at the last pew. A wave of reality gushed through my soul, and I heard a fiendish voice whisper, "You were a failure..." I rebuked it immediately, but I couldn't deny the realism of the situation.

I had let down a congregational member of mine, and I now had to take full culpability for her loss. I was frozen, standing motionless, my heart pounding, trying to escape from my chest.

As soon as I neared Blanca, I got down on my knees. I held her hands in mine, and I begged her for her forgiveness. I sobbed there for several long minutes.

Finally, after catching my breath, I looked up, and our eyes met. She too had tears running down her face, but her countenance was nowhere near sorrowful.

She placed her hands on my chin and lifted my face. With a gentle voice, she simply said, "Thank you."

She began to cry and smile and then laugh a little at the same time. She lifted my hand, indicating that I should stand up, as did she. Then, she hugged me tightly.

She began to chant, "Thank you, thank you, thank you..."

I was thoroughly confused. I pulled away and asked, "Ms. Blanca, why...? Why are you thanking me? I am in your debt. I am so sorry for—"

She cut me off, and with a peaceful smile, she said, "Darren wrote me a letter—a loving letter. He asked for forgiveness and told me that he loved me." She paused. "Most importantly, he told me that... he had found God in the desert."

She blew her nose and composed herself. "You see, I was suffering for years because my son was lost—lost in the wilderness of hatred and bitterness. And I've been praying for a long time, asking God that He would find my son, that God would change his heart and make it new, and that he would live out God's plan and purpose for his life.

"Here, let me show you, just a few weeks ago, he sent me a letter with these verses that had spoken to him in Isaiah 43:18-19:

> *18 Remember not the former things, nor consider the things of old. 19 Behold, I am creating a new thing in you, and now it will spring forth. Can you see it? I will make a way for your through the wilderness, and I will refresh you with streams in the desert.*

"Now, I could mourn this temporary loss, but I won't. I am choosing to rejoice that he found everlasting love and life with the King. I will see him again! I'm so glad you were able to befriend him and that his last moments were with a friend."

I couldn't hold it anymore. I broke down like an infant getting his first immunization shots. I realized then, I was the grieving member, and she was the pastor. God had restored her, in the most inconceivable way.

We hugged for the longest time, and I could feel such a loving embrace of gratitude. We sat and talked for about two hours about what Darren was like when he was young and how he shared his last moments with me—the progression and evolution of a caring young man. God had indeed created something new in Darren, and it was now being seen clearly by both his mother and me. We laughed. We cried some more. We rejoiced that we would see him again someday...

CHAPTER 28

~ Liberty and the Pursuit of Happiness ~

<u>Jordan</u>

After a few weeks home, although I loved being home with my girls, I missed doing God's work. I wanted to go back and help people. I felt better. I was ready. I could feel God tugging on my heart. It was time to go back to work. I knew it, and the girls knew it too.

I decided to appeal my medical clearance and continue my original assignment to Elmendorf. I prayed that God would give me a sign, to prove to myself and others that I was ready. Lo and behold, the phone rang about five minutes later.

It was Chaplain Dubose. "Jordan, we are having a few joint personnel from the Wing and the Pentagon visit us to overview our scheduled activities. I know you are on your time off, but you are my prime example to help vocalize to our upper commanders and explain why we need more chaplains and additional mental health assistance and resources. If you have the energy and strength to be here next week for a day or two, it would be appreciated."

I rolled my eyes and smirked a little, because as usual, even when I wasn't on duty, Dubose always "needed" me to do his work for him.

But I humbly accepted, knowing that the phone call had not been a coincidence and that this was my way to get my foot in the door.

Mental health awareness and making sure that soldiers that came back from deployment had more than enough resources to heal physically, mentally, emotionally, and spiritually was something that God was impressing deeply on my heart.

Perhaps all these things had happened as part of God's perfect plan to help in saving more broken souls from self-harm and death. Perhaps what I had gone through with the suicide of Robert Nunes and then experiencing PTSD firsthand had been preparing me so that lives could be saved. I was excited about the possibilities and what God had in store. I could hardly wait to tell Joanna about the phone call.

*****

A very anticipated Tuesday morning, I was glad to go back to work "officially", even if it was just only for one day. Wearing the uniform that came back with me brought a profound understanding of life and liberty. Sweat, tears, blood, brokenness, hope, happiness, love. I was free. That was what so much of the world was missing: liberty. Without liberty, there would continue to be conflicts that resulted in war. My job was to let the world know of the liberty offered by the ones who died for me.

After making sure every hair was in place and looking mighty good, if I did say so myself, I decided to head out and drive by myself to base. Joanna gave me her blessing, after asking a thousand times if I was sure that I was okay to drive.

I told her, "Eventually, the butterfly has to flap its wings, circulate motion, and learn to navigate on its own."

She laughed then—a happy lilting sound that echoed in my mind and in my heart.

*****

As I pulled into the chapel parking lot, I was iffy where I should park: the "chaplain" spot or "visitors". Then, I realized I still had my disability placard to park in the handicap space. I did it with no regrets, although my knee had healed very quickly, thanks to all the physical therapy.

I got my hat out and put it on. I took a deep breath, and I murmured "Godspeed" to myself. It was time to shine.

I approached Chaplain Dubose's office, and before I entered, I made sure to say hello to Sergeant Miller and the new faces that just PCS'd (Permanent Change of Station) here. The welcome was overwhelming and consoling. I told them all that it was nice to see them, but that I had to hurry on to the sanctuary, since everyone was there waiting for me to speak.

I keep on walking, hearing Chaplain Dubose voice in the hallway, via the speakers, about the history of this chapel, the pertinence and importance of chaplains... I entered the sanctuary and sat all the way in the back pews, signaling to him that I had arrived with a wave.

He saw me right away and changed his tune, redirecting the subject matter to me. "Well, well, well... speaking of chaplains, please let me introduce you to a great man who just came back from deployment. There, he had to witness the war's outtake on our men, spiritual and moral depletion, as well as life and death. I'm not going to get into specifics, but please stand with me as I'd like introduce Chaplain Ramonda."

Wow, what an introduction! I stood up a bit shakily, and I began to walk down the aisle. I was stopped intermittently by handshakes on both sides. It was a revered standing ovation, and right then, I felt God's exaltation. I fought the tears with all my might, and I began to shake nervously.

I saw many stars—general stars, colonels, lieutenant colonels, majors... all ranking officers. It was an honor and a very humbling moment. I took a deep breath, exhaled, and asked God for mercy, the right words to say, and for help in delivering His message.

Once up at the podium, I began, "Thank you, everyone. Please, please be seated." Everyone kept on clapping, so I bowed my head with humility and awe. I decided to wait until the claps died down.

After a few seconds, I resumed, "Thank you. I'm honored to be back here. This is what I do. This is what I love. This is what I live for. I was asked to talk about the shortage of chaplains and the shortage of mental health assistance and resources. As chaplains, we simply do not work just from 8-5pm. Our work is not fixed into time slots of the week, but it is subjective to the timing of the needs of individuals. We balance our family, work, and God's ministry as our holy trinity.

"We serve our active duty personnel and their spouses here at home—especially when spouses are deployed, and they need favors, child-care, etc. We service our retirees, veterans, widows, contract-personnel, and anyone that has access to the military installation.

"We are not like doctors, that are assigned to a specific unit and their family members in that squadron, that base, that state. We service anyone who flies in from any state who requests a funeral, benediction, promotion, etc. We prepare the time for an event, and sometimes must abruptly leave for an urgent call all in the same day.

"For example, one of the hardships of going into work would be visiting a family whose child died from cancer, crying with them, praying with them, and consoling the family. Then, immediately after, needing to rush to a promotional ceremony for a service member that is a celebration and a joyous occasion. Some days are an emotional roller coaster. We rely on our faith for regeneration, healing, sympathy, and any other emotional aspect to help others.

"We are short-staffed. We need more people to step up and become chaplains to alleviate the weight and emotional toll on other chaplains. Statistics show that chaplains have a higher percentage of high blood pressure, heart diseases, and other physical problems due to the emotional toll that has taken over their long careers.

"When an emergency occurs on base, they don't page the doctor, or JAG (Judge Advocate/Military Lawyer); they page us to be readily available and provide the assistance needed. We must acutely split our time between our family, work, and outside work hours. After God, family is what invigorates us to perform our best.

"A chaplain's day is supposed to be broken into 3 increments: 8 hours of rest, 8 hours of work, 8 hours of leisure. It saddens me when I give more time to work than my family because we are short-staffed. We need rest and our family to face this vicious world. My girls are my sword and shield to fall back on when situations go awry. They are my support staff. Time spent with them is essential for healing and rejuvenation.

"Now, I know plenty of single chaplains that solely rely on God 100% to face these encounters, but those who are committed in relationships have established a foundation of respect, communication, growth, and love, and it needs to be cared for in order to share it with those who seek that kind of relationship. You cannot give, what you don't have. I need love. I need peace. I need strength. I need a corvette..."

Everyone was shocked for a moment and then laughter began to erupt throughout the pews.

I continued, "I'm just kidding. I don't need a corvette. HA! My point is, just as I need physical rest for my body to function, chaplains also need mental, emotional, and spiritual rest. We intake and absorb emotions from bitter, sad, angry, jealous, vindictive people on a daily basis. We rely on our faith to combat those feelings and to keep them from seeping into our lives.

"We also have to prepare for the occasions in people's lives like weddings, promotions, ceremonies of any kind, hospital visits, funerals, speeches, sermons, family functions, marriage retreats, Bible studies, luncheons, and so much more! For us to continue these rituals, we need the tools and resources.

"A house of worship is to be maintained, to be honored, to be restored. People would feel more comfortable and inclined to visit a chapel that is kept clean, with bathrooms that work, seats that aren't torn, equipment that works, etc.

"I see all the time that our gyms get updated equipment, renovated areas, extensions. Just as some people choose to work on their bodies and maintain physical health, there are those who choose to work on their spiritual and emotional well-being. As chaplains, we are their coaches, because ultimately, it's up to them to reach their desired aspiration.

"Just as technology advances, every unit, every squadron, every agency needs to adapt and obtain new technology to better perform and complete their designated task/mission. The chapel isn't a still institution that should be omitted from the rest of the department of defense. Our mission is everywhere, with everyone.

"Please help us obtain better tools, better facilities, more resources, and additional assistants to complete the mission: to serve our members wholly with God's grace. Thank you all for coming. God bless you!"

I was met with another standing ovation throughout the half-filled chapel. I think I did okay. I wasn't entirely sure what I was going to say when I walked up to the podium. But, sometimes, I've found it works best not to over prepare and let God speak through me. I thanked God for giving me the opportunity to speak amongst the highest ranks, leaders, and authority figures.

I gathered my notes and began to walk down the aisle, but I was stopped by each officer to shake hands. Just as I was about to exit the chapel, I heard one of the new chaplain assistants yell towards me, "Sir! Um, Chaplain Ramonda! Wait! Aren't you going to stay for lunch? Chaplain Dubose was hoping you'd stay and speak with Colonel Kingsley, the head of the AFCCC?"

I smiled and said, "I appreciate the kind gesture and cordial invitation, but I just came to preach the Word. I just want to go home to my wife and family now."

With no words left to say, he nodded and respected my choice to leave. I realized that although I hadn't even been there for 30 minutes, they all witnessed the hollow shadow that followed me, the footpath of my strong will to continue this fight, and my hope and passion to finish God's mission.

CHAPTER 29

~ Beauty for Ashes ~

<u>Jordan</u>

Back in Texas, 4 Years Later...

As I parked the vehicle into the main lot, I couldn't help but admire the chapel... nothing had changed really, but I had. My time here had shaped me into a new creation.

My mind briefly wandered to all that had happened in the last 4 years...

I was on my last year at the assignment at Elmendorf AFB, and I was to be promoted to Lieutenant Colonel. Rebecca got accepted into her school of choice: Baylor University. Joanna got a job working at Lily's school as a Provost Administrator. We were all content. We were all happy with the way that God was working all things out together for good.

Things got even better when I got the news that I'd be returning here, once again in Texas for my next assignment, as the Wing Chaplain. I was excited to be close with Becca. And, just when I thought things couldn't get any better, I received a call asking me to officiate the wondrous wedding of Jennifer Nunes and Bryan Doherty.

So, here I found myself once again in my old parking spot in front of the chapel. Memories flashed through my mind—good and bad. I snapped out of it and focused on the moment. I was here, back with my family.

I was anxious to see her, for she was special. Without her, I technically wouldn't be here today, or alive. Today was special for her too... Ms. Blanca, God Bless her, had been asked to walk Jennifer down the aisle. Although it looked like it would never happen, she was able to participate and cherish love from others.

As I walked inside, I immediately went towards the private rooms in the back, to greet the special couple on their special day.

Wow. Jennifer looked stunning in her white dress, with Henry (now 7) by her side. She looked like she belonged to God, for she had given herself completely to Him. This was not the same Jennifer I knew 4 years ago.

Seeing her, I thought it would have brought back flashbacks, but it didn't. It really didn't. I felt peace. I couldn't help but think of my daughters, hoping that they too would give themselves to God.

I left Joanna and the girls to keep talking to Jennifer, calming her nerves, and I decided to go see Bryan.

We had kept in touch for years. We emailed back and forth for advice, suggestions, and the honor of joining them in union before God. It was all part of God's perfect timing, as I'd gotten back to Texas and settled in my new assignment.

I knocked on the door, and I heard a "Come in!" I opened the door, and there was Bryan with his 2 friends. I immediately shook their hands, and I gave Bryan a big bear hug.

It's was amazing how Bryan, too, had changed in 4 years. He looked surer of himself, and ever-so humble.

As I began talking to him, we heard a knock on the door. I turned around, and there she was. I smiled. Ms. Blanca. Our eyes met. With my body on autopilot, I walked towards her, and we embraced.

I had done many weddings as part of my job, but never had I looked forward to another one after my own. This wedding was going to be different.

We began to chat for a few minutes before I excused myself to head toward the sanctuary and prepare myself for the ceremony. The beautiful flowers that concealed the old, chipped pews reminded me of how something beautiful can come from brokenness.

As I began to look over my notes of what I would be saying, I felt a tap on my shoulder from one of the ushers. They were ready to begin the ceremony.

I heard the music wind down, and a reverent hush fell over the crowd. I moved into position on the stage, standing in front of the podium instead of behind it, to give a more personal feeling. From where I was standing, I could see my beautiful Joanna sit down with the girls. There wasn't a "his" side or "her" side on the pews; it was a combination of all.

The processional song "Here Comes the Bride" began. Bryan turned around, his face beaming with joyous emotion.

From a distance, I couldn't really see Jennifer's face, but I could see the glow on Ms. Blanca's. They both seemed to glide down the aisle. Ms. Blanca's arm was proudly entwined with Jennifer's.

Death and sadness had come to these two women, but it did not conquer. Love now birthed a new beginning in their lives.

I quickly and silently offered a prayer of praise and gratitude for all the Lord had done.

Once more my eyes landed on the beautiful Serbian phoenix flowers, adorning the rugged, oak pews, and I smiled. I set my notes aside. I didn't need them. This was a marriage blessed by God, and He would guide me with the right words to say.

I opened my Bible to Isaiah 61:3, and began to read out loud:

"...for He will give them beauty for ashes, joy for mourning, and praise for sadness. They shall be called oaks of righteousness, that the Lord has planted, so that He will be glorified through them..."

I paused then, just briefly, to smile first at Bryan, then Jennifer, and my eyes met Joanna's before continuing. My heart beat deeply in my chest with excitement over what the Lord had planned for the next chapter in our lives.

Epilogue
~ Demoted To A Higher Rank ~

Rebecca

Five years later...

"I do"—the oral signature of acceptance and agreement. I married my best friend, Ray. We were about to embark on a new journey together as husband and wife, as active duty member and spouse.

I was no longer the melodramatic teen I used to be. Before, I sat back and watched before my eyes the videography of my life: the support my mother gave my father, the patience, sacrifices, tears, and the great energy that it took her to help revitalize his days, weeks, and journeys. I was no longer going to be the backseat passenger, with time on my hands, having nothing better to do than to watch the scenes unfold before my eyes. Now, I was going to be the driver of my destiny, helping to make decisions, waiting on a turn, letting others pass, or sometimes even cutting ahead if that's what was needed.

I would no longer put myself first, for I had made a vow to Ray, my dear husband. He brought me such joy. He made me happy. He was the reason I knew of the unconditional love of God Almighty.

I loved Ray with all of me, and I would do my very best to be worthy of his love. I feared disappointing him. God knew of my imperfections, weaknesses, and fallouts, so He gave me Ray—my equal value, yet my leader. I didn't want him at first, but God unveiled I needed him, and truly, I do.

*****

It was 9:12 am, and I was running late to get to the Personnel Office because I had been battling oncoming traffic. As usual, parking availability was virtually nonexistent, and I resorted to parking in another departmental area.

It never failed; I could almost always count on a long walk when on a military base. I did my best to speed walk as fast as I could and ignore my surroundings. But, my mind wandered as I raced. All the buildings look the same: ugly brown. I wondered if the buildings were painted yellow or orange if maybe people would look forward to coming into work. Vibrant hues shouted excitement, dull colors were deemed depressing and dispirited.

When I finally arrived at the Personnel Office, I had to wait in line to be seen. I took one last look at my military ID. "United States Uniformed Services" it read. I quickly inspected the card and noticed that it was in mint condition, rarely used. It stated: "Identification and Privilege Card", and I thought about what those words really meant. *Privileges? How about all the suffering? Time spent apart? Tears? Headaches and heartaches?*

There wasn't a full disclaimer on what one was really signing up to do. I didn't serve the Armed Forces; I was going to serve my husband so that he could succeed in the Air Force. It was kind of amusing how a small, tangible item could bring back derivative memories. I took a deep breath, as I heard my number getting called out. I submitted all the marital documentation to the technician and quickly sat on the chair, while fixing my hair for the photo shoot.

As I finish grooming my hair, I quickly looked at my compact mirror to make sure my teeth were in order. As I put all my things away, I patiently waited for the technician to input all the information into the computer.

I looked around the office and began to wonder why it was so bland: no pictures, no décor, no self-expression, no identity... how ironic.

"Ma'am, are you ready?" the tech asked, interrupting my thoughts.

"Yes, yes, I am," I responded. I sat, looked straight towards the camera, and smiled.

"Oh, no, I didn't mean for the camera," she explained. "I meant, are you ready to turn in your old ID?"

I quickly dug into my pocket and looked at it one last time. I handed it over to her. She glanced at it and chuckled a bit.

Embarrassed, I tried to beat her to the punchline, "Yes, yes, I know. I was much younger in that picture. I know; I'm old."

She shook her head and replied, "No, no, no! Dear, you're lovely. I just think it's funny you had under "Sponsor Rank" showing as "Lieutenant Colonel", and now your new ID will show your sponsor rank as simply "Lieutenant". Girl, you've been demoted!"

I never thought of it that way, but I shrugged it off with a fake smile and looked away. She noticed her comment may not have sat well with me, and she continued, "...but, to a better position, you are now a spouse!"

Her attempt to neutralize the tension faded. She took the photo and began to print it out. She briefly smiled and said, "Please sign here on the signature mark."

I used my best possible cursive handwriting, and I returned the paper to her. She cut out the picture, processed it into a lamination printer, and then sealed it properly.

She looked at it one last time and handed it to me. "Here you go, Mrs. Celeste. Have a great journey."

I replied with a sincere, "Thank you."

I walked back to my car slowly, lost in thought. Once I got back in my car, before I decided to drive away, I quickly took out the newly printed ID to check it out.

In disbelief, I began to grasp the enormity of the whole new journey before me. I had just signed up to be part of the military again, but I was better prepared and knew what to expect for this position. I was no longer a child, dependent of a sponsor, but a spouse! Because of the Godly example my parents had set for me and because of God's grace and perfect plan, waiting patiently for my life's purpose was finally paying off. I had been officially demoted to a higher rank!

~ About the Author ~

Ruth Lee Alfred was born in Bayamon, Puerto Rico and was raised in Orlando, FL and San Antonio, TX. She currently resides in Florida with her active duty husband, Michael, and their two sons, Caleb & Jacob.

~ **Biographical Facts** ~

- While most enlisted folks get ready to retire after 20 years of service at the age of 38, my father joined the military at the age of 39. Many doubted his admission due to health issues, age, and language barriers. His faith has surpassed all those obstacles, and he is still active duty, set to retire in 2022.
- I attended 3 high schools, 2 in different states. My grades did slip, due to bitterness, but eventually, I was able to redeem myself. My parents did buy me that car...
- If I hadn't left the comfort zone of my family in my homeland of Puerto Rico, I wouldn't know the bigger opportunities presented and the blessings God had in store for me. Let go of the known and embrace God's path to the unknown, for it will always surpass your expectations!
- I told God that I didn't want to marry anyone from the military, let alone one of my brother's friends. I met my husband at the Air Force Academy, and I've gone from living (as a preacher's daughter) with one that prays to the heavens to now (married) living with one that flies in them...

Tell God your plans!

As Iron Sharpens Iron

So One Person Sharpens Another

Proverbs 27:17

Manufactured by Amazon.ca
Bolton, ON